Mary Perkins Ives Abbott

Alexia

Mary Perkins Ives Abbott

Alexia

ISBN/EAN: 9783337225995

Printed in Europe, USA, Canada, Australia, Japan

Cover: Foto ©Andreas Hilbeck / pixelio.de

More available books at **www.hansebooks.com**

BY

MARY ABBOTT

CHICAGO

A. C. McCLURG AND COMPANY

1889

PREAMBLE.

I COULD not fill one page with the romance of my own life, to save that prosy existence; it is as empty of any such claim upon public attention as a stubble-field is barren of wheat. One reason for this may be that I have another self, — a friend, — whose joys and sorrows, hopes and fears, have been more than mine, and have left me no time for private ventures of my own in those lines. For this man required more looking after than a child, and was not half so tractable. He used to remind me — great, handsome, impossible fellow that he was — of nothing so much as a splendid, full-rigged, A 1 clipper ship, lacking a course and a captain. When such a craft slips her cable, and takes to the high seas, somebody must steer. I used to act as sailing-master sometimes, when I saw the vessel making straight for big rocks or sunken reefs; and although I did not always see the danger in time to prevent the ship from being badly strained, actual wreck was averted while I had the helm.

Certain chapters in this man's history have not been without their pathos, and cannot fail, as I guess and hope, to interest the human, — those who sin and are sorry, and sin and are sorry, and sin and are sorry yet again. So, as I know that he would never put pen to paper, to jot down one word himself, I, Felix Farley, the awkward scribe, attempt the task, making this preface both my apology and plea.

ALEXIA.

I.

WHEN Geoffrey Trevor was thirty years old, he committed an act — a crime I was nearly going to call it — of which I could not have suspected him, and for which I never forgave him. He became engaged to be married.

If he had fallen in love first, — a not uncommon preliminary, — nobody would have been more rejoiced than I, for in that case marriage might have been his making. But he had done nothing of the kind ; I knew it, and he knew I knew it. There was no pretence of love about the matter.

If you ask what was the motive for this absurd deed, I do not refer you to his flimsy reasons, which were no reasons at all, but I answer simply, I don't know.

My experience, I may say here, has taught
me, that for rash, unthinking perform-
ances of this description, you may com-
mend yourself, as a rule, to gentlemen who
have nothing on earth to do but to plan
them. That was Geoffrey's case to a turn.

There are men whom Fortune has bored
to the verge of extinction with her favors ;
and Geoffrey Trevor was one of these.
Born with a silver spoon in his mouth, and
half-a-dozen fairy godmothers, he had been
surfeited with sweets, until his appetite
had first palled, then perished, by what it
had fed on. And if the laying down of
his life (I quote his own sentiment now)
had not involved more loathing, in antici-
pation of the nuisance it would have en-
tailed upon others, than the bearing of it
already did, in fulfilment, to himself, he
would have been, not glad exactly, for pri-
mary emotions were gone for him, but
willing enough to shuffle it off, and have
done with it. Hardly the tone of a
rapturous wooer, if I understand such
things.

Helen Courtice, a magnificent, proud
creature in Geoffrey's set, happened to be

the girl he chose thus to " honor." I say happened, for there would have been equal fitness in the selection if it had fallen upon any one of twenty others, all of the same pattern, with whom Geoffrey had been in the habit of spending much time before his latest season of misanthropy had set in.

I was fearfully shocked when I heard this news about Geoffrey, and at first I refused to believe it. For it was not three days since Geoffrey had come to me in one of his blackest, bitterest moods. He said that he believed his blood was drying up in his veins; that he felt no sensations, either of pleasure or of pain; that he neither liked nor disliked anything nor anybody; that he was incapable of feeling hungry or thirsty, hot or cold; that with the exception of a kind of instinctive clinging to me and tobacco and sleep he might as well be a mummy; and that if he had had spirit enough to wish a wish, he should wish he was one. And with these jocund words, he had thrown himself upon my sofa, in a favorite attitude, — his hands clasped behind his head, eyes shut, and an expression of utter weariness upon his face. He meant, or thought he meant, every syllable of this chant of woe. He was getting into the worst kind of way; and this thing must be stopped.

"Now come, Geoff Trevor," I said to him, severely, "I am about worn out with this nonsense; you talk like a fool, and you will be one soon, if you keep on. The matter with you is that you 're spoiled by good fortune; you have always had too much time, too much money, too much looks, and too much attention. You 're moping and whining now because the last doll is stuffed with saw-dust, I suppose. What is it, — a horse you 've bet on, or a girl you 're deceived in? For Heaven's sake, write a book; 'get religion;' fall in love; go into politics, — do something to get yourself out of this slough, or upon my word, old boy, you 'll be found dead of nothing but the dumps!"

He was lying motionless, in the old attitude, on the couch.

I went on. "I wish, with all my heart, you were as poor and as ugly as I am; you 'd have to go to work, then, and women would n't trouble you any more. A month of severely-let-alone-ness at the Club, when you 're languidly looking for Mrs. Van Uxem's scented summons to her Metropolitan Arcadia, would make you open those blasé orbs a little; and a few snubs would perhaps give you a zest for your next invitation, if you ever got one. As it is, your table is piled high at this moment with notes of urgency, I dare swear; and it bores you even to execrate the writers, while you concoct civil answers."

I said all this with what I meant for a stinging sneer. I seldom talk so much at a time, and stopped to take breath, — for I had by no means finished, — when Geoffrey took his hat, and walked toward the door, saying, " I suppose you *are* sick of my everlasting moaning ; but you 're the biggest bore I have to contend with when you talk against time."

I hoped he was angry, for a good quarrel would have been a tonic for him ; but he lounged back, and threw himself into a big chair, with apathy written all over him. I was preparing another verbal torpedo, when he spoke again.

"Politics!" he muttered, "politics! Did n't I try electioneering one year, and did n't it take me three months to get the dirt off my hands, and six, off my soul, — if it 's ever come off, which I 'm not so sure of? If there is a clean calling, show it me, and I 'll begin on it to-morrow. I don't know one. I have tried writing, as you know, and failed. I tell you, Felix, mentally I am a corpse."

"Well, you can't learn an honest trade then, any more than a dishonest; and the only advice I can give you is to come and read law in my office again, and make up your mind to stick to it." He had made beginnings before, but had always gone away, or something, and given it up.

Geoffrey shook his head. "It's no use," he said, "to try to do anything for me, old man, but I won't come here and make a nuisance of myself again."

Well, we talked nearly all night, but I could do Geoff no good; he had strange fancies about himself and his moods, and was altogether in a worse condition than I had supposed. I could see that it was all owing to his lack of training, and listless life, and that he had no real mental disease. He was sure he had one of an alarming kind.

I fell asleep in my chair at last, and when I woke up, I heard the wheels of his cab driving away.

You may now conceive my amazement at hearing, only three days after this orgy, of Geoffrey's choice of an " honest calling." He sauntered in soon to tell me of it, or to hear what I had to say. Of course he knew I had heard.

I never minced matters with Geoffrey Trevor, but always spoke my mind out flat·· to him ; and that was one reason, I think, for his liking me. "They all lie to me but you, Felix," he used to say; "if you ever do it, my last hope is gone." I had occasion afterward to wonder if he was always implicitly truthful to me.

Well, Geoffrey came in one day, soon after the announcement of his strange performance, trying to look very easy and casual, but I soon bowled him out of that.

" You 're not engaged, are you, Geoff ? " I burst forth the very first thing, before he had time to open his mouth, thus ridding him of all embarrassment in beginning, at least.

" Yes, I am," he said, reddening, " and to a charming girl too. Won't you wish me joy, my boy, eh?" I never saw such hang-dog mirth in my life; he looked like a sheep-stealer.

" Sit down!" I said, in a voice like thunder. " Are you in your senses? Don't you know that after all you have told me about yourself, you are committing a crime in rushing into a thing like this pell-mell, even if it were decent to do it in any case? A man in your mental state — if what you have told me is true — has no right to marry. Suppose one of those 'numb' fits comes on, such as you have told me about, lasting for days, during which time you have absolutely not one particle of human sympathy, nothing but disgust for your kind, what's your wife going to do then? Are you about to sacrifice a woman to your whims, or disorders, or whatever they are?"

Geoffrey was white and angry. He stopped me. "I have told you always to speak freely to me, Felix, but even you can't insult me. Everything I have told you about myself is true, of course ; from living like an imbecile, I have grown to be one. I have looked after my own comfort so keenly that I have overshot the mark ; but I am going to lead another life altogether. My mother was anxious that I should marry Helen Courtice ; my relations all wish it now ; so do hers."

I was glad to find him so thoughtful of his relations ; he usually alluded to them as " brutes ! "

" Helen is a beautiful woman ; she has accomplishments, is sweet-tempered, and likes me. The noble passion we neither of us affect, to any extent ; but as I believe there is really no such thing, it would be only a pretence if we did. We have as great a liking for each other as persons have when they marry, I suppose. As for the attacks of which I spoke to you, and which you have seen fit to ridicule, occupation will be a cure for them ; and you may be very sure that no woman under my protection shall suffer from my neglect. I shall try to make a good husband.

As I have never seen one, it will be a novelty to create the part."

"Geoff," I shouted, "for Heaven's sake go and break this fearful thing off! Tell her you have made a mistake, or she has; tell her anything; but don't pile guilt on your unhappiness. Don't make a hopeless fool of yourself; don't wreck two lives! The girl will get over it now; but never if you marry her. And O Geoff! think of *your* misery! Come, give it up!" And I seized his arm.

He gave a quick little laugh of impatience, and shook me off nervously. "Very flattering all this, to the lady," he said. "I am the luckiest man about, to win such a prize; everybody says so. She may throw me over when she finds what a dullard I am, but I have ceased to have any right to act, even if I wished it; and of course I don't."

I tried him at other points; but he had a parry for every thrust. I could have roared for very unhappiness. As for bettering his blues, or whatever they were, he had simply jumped from the frying-pan into the fire. What could bore you more, if you come to that, than to be tied to a woman you neither love, respect, nor admire particularly, only like " as much as most persons like when they marry ! " It was horrible !

After Geoffrey Trevor's and Helen Courtice's engagement had been discussed to infinity, and dined to death, and buried in flowers, and everything had quieted down, and Geoffrey was behaving beautifully, the young woman made the worst move she could possibly have acquitted herself of, under the circumstances, — she went abroad. They had been engaged then about three months, and there really seemed to be a prospect of their being happy, after a fashion, in time. Helen flirted still, and always would do that ; but Geoffrey never minded a bit, and could have had the same privilege himself, I dare say. He was devoted to her, and for a restless woman of fashion, she seemed contented. Geoffrey drove with her, rode with her, walked with her, dined and " balled " where she would, without flinching. He spoke of her to me in affectionate enough terms, and seemed proud of her beauty. It was generally conceded that he was a pattern lover ; and he seemed to be growing cheerful, and quite like other men, when that little fool started up a European trip!

"It's ages since I was in Paris," she said; "why can't we go over and spend May and June there, and go to Homburg for July and August? Mamma would like nothing better; my cousins the Lorimer men will go; the Leonards are already there; you will like it, Geoffrey, of course; and—"

Geoffrey shook his head.

"Do you mean to say you won't go, Geoffrey Trevor? *May* I be allowed to ask why, when you know very well you haven't an earthly thing to keep you here? Oh, that stupid old house! That can wait, I'm sure. Do you really mean you *won't go*, Geoffrey?" And Helen looked black and cross.

Now Geoffrey was, for the first time in his life, employed upon something which absorbed him. He was building a house for Helen, and was putting his whole heart into the work. I could have killed that girl for not seeing — or for not caring, rather — how important this occupation was to Geoffrey, and how much good it was doing him. But she had never understood, nor tried to understand, one thing about Geoffrey. She took all his devotion for granted, and gave him nothing, or very little, in return. As for her, there was nothing to understand about her except her selfishness and her worldly ambition. Yes, and her obstinacy, — I forgot that, — for Helen was like a mule when she had set her head — she had no heart — upon doing a thing. "You know how dull the summers are here, Geoffrey dear," she said, plying another weapon, "even at Newport. I'm sure I hate it, with the same everlasting women scanning one's gowns! And of course this year, just before I get my trousseau" (here she slid her hand into Geoffrey's and managed to blush a little), "I sha'n't have any new ones."

"Then they won't scan you," answered Geoffrey. "If it's a question of gowns, you shall have a thousand, if you will stay at home and be married, like a good girl, and won't go away and leave me." I think he was positively afraid to let her go. "This is the first time I have ever tried to do a piece of real work, Helen," he said to her, earnestly, "and I must not leave it, es-

pecially in this state. I beg you will see
the thing sensibly."

Whether Helen saw it sensibly or in-
sensibly, she went. Geoffrey, firm in his
refusal, saw them all off, — a jolly, careless
lot, — and came to my rooms that night,
thoroughly discouraged, and about as bad
as ever.

II.

I FOUND there was a feeling — if a fashionable set can be said to have feeling, a kind of ripple, at any rate — of disapproval of Helen Courtice's conduct, in leaving Geoffrey at this juncture and going away for the summer.

It was not so much disapproval, either, — nothing so moral, — as a sense that she had done a foolish thing for herself. Geoffrey Trevor was known to be a peculiar man, — although no mortal but me knew how peculiar, — and it would not be easy for any woman to hold his affection, except at the short end of the lever. She was very silly to leave him behind, her friends said, even if she did want to flirt with Max Lorimer all summer, — how silly they all one day would find out!

I was lunching with Geoffrey at the Club, about a fortnight after Miss Courtice had sailed away, when Geoff's cousin Murray

Trevor, the only relation he knew much
of, came up to us. He was looking for
Geoff, he said ; one or two men had told
him that Geoff was getting hipped and
sour. " I want you to go down to Quartz
with me to-night, my boy," he said. " No
noes taken and no questions asked."
Quartz Point was a small peninsula, well
known to yachtsmen, but sparsely inhab-
ited, where Murray had a house. "Laura
has ordered me to bring you, and if I appeared without you, I should n't be let in.
So meet me at the station, at five o'clock
sharp ; if I don't find you, I shall miss the
train, and come up after you." Geoffrey
laughed, and said he should n't be there.
I persuaded him to go, however, and he
went.

The day after Geoffrey had gone down
to Quartz Point with his cousin, I met him
coming from the train. He said he was
going down again that night, and he drew
a very attractive picture of the rough
beauty of the place, — all rocks and shingle and surf on one side, the sea side, he
said (I had never been there) and on the
other the old fishing town of Quartz

Head, with its irregular outline, stretching the length of a bold bluff, and overlooking the basin, or harbor, which lay between the Point and itself. The sunset over and behind the old town was marvellous; and there was a perfectly lovely young girl, granddaughter of Murray's old fisherman, who rowed them over the harbor the night before, and back this morning, when they went to take the train at Quartz Head. I should have guyed him about the girl, it was so uncommon a thing for him to notice one in that condition of life, but any earthly object which could rouse interest, to say nothing of enthusiasm, in Geoffrey, was a godsend, and I would not for the world have discouraged him!

I did not see Geoffrey very often at this period; but when I did, he was always just "running down to Quartz," or just "running up from Quartz." He stayed down three or four days at a time, often, and once he stayed a week, I believe.

I noticed the most wonderful improvement, or series of improvements, in Geoffrey, whenever I saw him. He looked the image of health; his eyes were eager and

animated; and he walked off like a boy.
I had never seen him so in my life before;
and I began to be curious to visit a place
which could work such miracles.

He was wild about Quartz Point; it
was all kinds of beauty combined, he told
me; that is to say, not the Point itself
wholly, but taking in all its surroundings.
The most charming spot he had ever
seen.

Now Quartz Point was by no means an
unknown region, although I, who stick to
my books, and who seldom sail, had never
happened to see it. It was hardly twenty
miles from town, and was well known, as I
have said, to yachtsmen, possessing, as it
did, a safe little harbor with neither bar
nor tide-way, — so much frequented by
them, in fact, as to have a yacht club-
house upon it. Geoffrey must have been
there a hundred times, before this year.
"Why is Quartz Point so surprisingly new
to you?" I asked him; "it's not possible
these are your first visits there?" Oh, he
said, he had been there sailing, of course,
and had anchored in the harbor, and had
dined at the Club; but he had never stayed

with Murray before, nor seen the place to any advantage. " Murray is quite lord of the land, and the townspeople worship him. They are most interesting studies, those rough old fishermen, Felix. The sailing is perfection ; I have n't seen a fog yet, contrary to tradition. [Well, he would, if he waited long enough.] And as for the sunsets, Italy never produced a patch upon them."

Geoffrey Trevor an enthusiast ! I should expect the sunset to fall on him next !

We had few and short opportunities for conversation in those days ; but by and by I got nearer the gist of it. " What do you think I have been doing this morning ?" he asked me once, coming into my office.

"Oh, tell," I said ; for I hate guessing.

" Buying a *dress*," he answered.

"For Mrs. Trevor ?" Murray's wife, I meant.

" No."

" Well, then ? "

" For a little girl."

" How big a little girl ?" I was getting suspicious.

"Oh, I don't know; sixteen or seventeen, perhaps."

"Ah, indeed. And how do you happen to be selecting young ladies' wardrobes? Rather new business for you, is n't it?"

"It is n't a young lady — I mean she's not grown-up, exactly; she's the granddaughter of Murray's fisherman and factotum, old Iron. [Hm! the perfectly lovely young girl who had rowed him over the first night he had gone down!] Such a character he is too, Felix! I wish you could hear some of his speeches. Laura has them by heart. What do you suppose he said to her the other day? 'Mrs. Treevor,' he said, rolling his tongue out, and drawing it in again, and smacking his lips, — all this between every two sentences, — 'my wife hes hed the eye-complaint, an' now she's got the spinal disease; an', Mrs. Tree-vor, ef you was to set two boatloads of gold before that woman, she could not unbutton her shoes!'"

I laughed very much at this; partly because it amused me, partly to encourage Geoff, and mostly for joy at seeing the change in him.

But the little girl of seventeen and the dress, I wanted to hear more about them. So I asked Geoffrey if the infant he had bought the dress for was as amusing as her grandfather.

"Oh," he exclaimed hastily, and a look I did n't know came into his face, "she's of another race altogether; a being from another world; an Undine with her soul, — in one way an enigma; in a second, a perfectly transparent, simple creature."

I had seen artless country girls before, and knew what they were like. I could n't help smiling in my sleeve at this cynic, caught by cunning.

"She was sent to her grandfather by his son, a miserable, sneaking scamp, who had disappeared before that, for years, — the only kind thing he had ever done for his father."

"Except sending Undine," I broke in.

The autocrat frowned. "Do you want me to go on, or not?"

"Why, I want you to go on, of course, 'Mimosa,'" I retorted. "I am deeply thrilled."

And I was. I was glad to see that he

was coming round to be like other men, and was making an ass of himself. A silly little giggling country wench might well bear a bruise or two for this.

"Well, this wretch," Geoffrey went on, watching me rather sharply to see that I did n't chaff him again, "was sentenced to prison for thieving, or something, about ten years ago, and sent the child to the grandfather, who was so poor then he was almost supported by the town. The mother was unable to keep her, I suppose, or dead, or sentenced to jail too, perhaps. I don't know. Old Iron had never heard that his son was married even, until this child came to him."

"Perhaps he was n't," I remarked dryly.

"Perhaps not," Geoff sighed. "The poor girl's pedigree is of the darkest, I judge. The father has probably died, for he has never turned up."

"The girl is beautiful, you say?"

"She is not only marvellously lovely in face, but in character. She has quick intelligence, acute sensibilities, wit, and a sweet nature. She is merry at times without being noisy, sad at others without being solemn. As for her beauty, I never saw such eyes, to begin with, — eyes so full of soul and sympathy and earnestness, to say nothing of their actual splendor! She has the voice of an Englishwoman, and a smile like the sunrise. I am absolutely not exaggerating, Felix, and you know how fastidious I am."

Fastidious! I should say he was! A voice pitched a quarter of a semitone too high would disgust him with a woman, or the faintest glimmer of a gleam of imperfection in manner. But of course he was not comparing this rowing-girl with town-bred ladies, only speaking of her as a type apart. Yet listen to him now!

"I used to think it was with women as with music and drawing, and all those things. Every year there are better methods, and performers have to keep up with the times or drop out. They have to compete with the best talent going. A woman who does n't look after her looks, so to speak, constantly, has no show with the others. So, naturally, you don't expect to find your own sort of beauty — the beauty which alone satisfies you, I mean —

out of your own sphere. But here comes a girl who has none of the adjuncts we think indispensable; out in the sun and wind all day long; wears an old flannel gown of no color at all, just sewed together by a country dressmaker, I should think; still the most beautiful girl, out and out, I ever saw. By Jove, Felix, I can't find a flaw in her!"

"She must be amazing, then! I wish I could see her. Is that her grandfather's real name — no, it can't be! *Iron?* It's too absurd!"

"I don't know — no — yes — I believe so. I don't talk to her much about her descent, naturally; but somebody — Murray, I dare say — told me the grandfather was of foreign stock, — Portuguese, I think, — and his own name in that language meant iron; so they called him by it, as a joke first, and then it gradually grew to be his name. Solomon Iron, his name is," he continued; "awful, isn't it?"

"Monstrous. What's the name of the girl?"

"Alice; but the Sisters have given her the name of Alexia. It's the Greek for

Alice, and suits her wonderfully. I call
her by it."

" Then she is not an only child ? "

" Yes, she is ; I said so, did n't I ? They
would n't be apt to ship a numerous
family, one by one, in that mysterious
way."

" But you just said her sisters called her
Alexia."

" No, no, stupid ; *the* Sisters — of charity,
or mercy, or whatever they are ; both, in
this case, I should think. There are two of
them, — a kind of offshoot of some English
city sisterhood, doing mission work in the
town of Quartz Head. And they have
taught this girl for years."

"Oh ! " I began to see. " She's a
Catholic, of course ? "

" A *Catholic*, but not a *Roman* Catholic ! [This with mock dignity.] These
are sisters of the Anglican Church, — *the
true* church ; what you in your ignorance call the Episcopal, my boy. It's
the High Church movement, you know, —
priests and vestments and Eucharistic
lights and confession, and all the rest
of it."

"And have you gone to this church, or chapel, or whatever it is?"

"I? Oh yes, I go often. It's so pretty and solemn and interesting [O Geoff! what a combination!], and I sing a little, to help them out, as they're not rich enough to have a choir. Yes, I go; I'm rather regular."

He never put his nose inside a church at home.

"Oh, you are? You and 'Alexia' sing out of the same hymn-book, I suppose?"

"Oh, keep still, Felix," he retorted; "what a fool I am to tell you anything about the girl! I shall never hear the last of it!"

But *I* did; for he wouldn't open his lips on the subject again!

III.

IT was my fate, it seemed, always to be worrying about Geoffrey Trevor. Those few weeks I had been easier, seeing him so improved; and now that I knew the cause of the change, I was more bothered than ever! He was interested, through and through, in this young girl, whose beauty had been only the pioneer, I knew, in attracting him; for Geoffrey was no slave to looks, with nothing behind them. He was interested, now that he found himself, as he believed, a help and benefit to a human being; it was the work he had always, unknown to Geoffrey Trevor, been wanting. Here it was at his hand, and he was happy. A dangerous edged-tool kind of happiness for the girl, that was all.

Yes, this Undine with her soul, what of her? Was anybody looking after her? It was evident I had been mistaken in my estimate of her: she was no ogling, rustic lass, with her clumsy wiles, — I might have known no such could have held Geoffrey's attention for a minute, — but she was mistress of no practised arts, that was plain; and the disadvantage, in this unequal contest, was all hers. For Geoffrey, though in no sense a deceiver, except of himself, had not been a keen observer of the world's tierce and carte, without learning a few passes. We do some things unconsciously.

Of course I foresaw the inevitable, if indeed I were not looking back upon it; for the more I thought it over, the more I felt convinced that the inevitable had come to pass already. Undine would be, at any rate, if she were not then, in love with her Huldbrand! I have not described Geoffrey; he was a tall fellow, handsome and manly. And although I have represented him largely in his sulks, I was the only person to whom he showed this gloomy side; to the world he was a singularly attractive, more, a fascinating man. He had a fetching, tender, intense way with women,— put on, I used to tell him;

but when he cordially admired, as he did
this poor waif, it would be natural. How
could she withstand him, even his looks,
his manner? I can't describe Geoffrey's
features; I don't even know the color of
his eyes, but I do know that they were
declared to be dangerously effective organs
of vision. And I have heard women use
the same extravagant terms in speaking
of his appearance which he had employed
in depicting that of his wonderful new-
found beauty at Quartz Head, — at least,
such of them as might be applicable to
manly charms, or adapted in such a manner as to make them so.

There was sharp suffering ahead for
Geoffrey, who was always a fierce penitent
when the mischief was done. Nobody
ever slammed the barn-door as hard as he
after the horse was stolen, or ran so hotly
in pursuit of the abducted steed when he
was convinced it had actually gone. When
he found out that he had this innocent
young thing's heart concealed about his
person, his old misery, which after all was
general and impersonal, would seem like
happiness, compared to the new. When

he realized — as he would be the very last to do — that he had led this girl on, — and from his own tale, he was doing this at a hand-gallop, — what pangs would not be his forever more !

What would Geoffrey do, when he found out what he *had* done ? He would marry the girl in a minute, if he could, — for Geoffrey was noble in expiation, — but he could n't, because he was as good, or as bad, as married already ; and he would be quite as conscientious about his duty to Helen as he had been reckless in rushing into it, — more so, if anything ; for he had never loved Helen, and owed her reparation for that, to begin with.

What a miserable muddle it was ! My head ached worrying over it, and wondering what in fury was to be done.

I was in for it, that was a foregone conclusion ! I never was in a scrape of my own in my life ; I have n't the "go," or whatever is necessary, to get into them ; but hang me if I had ever been *out* of Geoffrey's ! I was profane at this epoch ; nothing but strong language kept me up. Some men (they say), take to strong drink when they are bothered; I always content myself with "big, big D.'s" of another description. The effects are more transient, and they do not, as a rule, bear witness against themselves.

I carefully arranged to run against Murray Trevor, — quite by accident, of course, — and I congratulated him upon the change in Geoffrey.

"He does look better, does n't he?" he said, with a quick smile. Murray's smile, I found, was quicker than his perception. " He 's as happy as a king down at Quartz, and quite the boy again. Only he never was a boy, so it has all the charm of freshness to him. He 's an eccentric chap, very, is n't he? Goes off by himself all the time, and has queer notions. I can't say I understand him; and I can't say I 've ever liked him, until this year. But then I 've never known him. My wife was vexed at Helen Courtice's leaving him in the lurch, so she thought we 'd better look after him a bit. You know he 's awfully 'gone' on Helen, and was blue as death at first. But he 's looking up a bit now."

Looking up! I should say he was. Then

Murray knew nothing of the maiden with the Greek name, and the Portuguese grandfather? If Geoffrey had been sly about the thing, I should be less lenient toward him.

"He said the fisher-people over at Quartz Head interested him," I ventured to say cautiously; "especially one old man and his family, — Iron, or some such name. He was telling me amusing anecdotes of them."

"Oh, yes, old Iron is a kind of servant of ours, — a queer, superannuated fisherman. Laura and I discovered Quartz Point years ago, when it had only a lighthouse and one other on it; and the first object we spied was old Iron, sitting on a rock, all doubled up, like a chimpanzee. We got him to row us across the harbor, and he's been doing it, off and on, ever since. He has a grandchild, who ferries for him, now he's got so old; the Sisters of the convent have looked after her and kept her in all these years. She's the handsomest girl you ever saw, and intelligent, and lovely altogether; quite a character in the little town, and has a hard history."

"Geoff said she was very beautiful."

"Oh, Geoff was regularly stunned, when he first saw her; he raves about her. And no wonder, either, she's so remarkable. Now look here, Farley," he said, stopping short, "you've never seen our little bluff, have you? Well, come down with us on Saturday, and see it for yourself. We'll go down early and go out sailing, and I'll show you all the points, including the village beauty,— Mrs. Trevor, of course, I mean," he added, laughing. "It's quiet as death, and in a way primitive, but that you'll like, as we do. And Laura will be awfully glad to see you."

I wasn't sure how awfully glad Geoff would be to see me, but I said I would go, with much joy. It was just what I wanted. I didn't see Geoffrey again until we found him swinging his legs over the edge of Blynn's wharf, at Quartz Head, on the Saturday. He was smoking, and looked the picture of calm content. I fancied he had not been away from the place for some days.

Geoffrey, I am sure, did not suspect why I had come to Quartz; my intimacy with

him accounted for Murray's asking me.
He had come over in a little tender to take
us on board Murray's sloop, which was
ready for us, with its mainsail flapping.
We sailed down the Willowby shore first;
misty and purple and beautiful it was,
with its Rhine-like castles towering over
the trees, and its more modestly placed
yet equally majestic villas, hiding behind
them; and then we stood ten miles out to
sea. I caught the charm of the place at
once; it was the air of life with which my
lungs were filling. Geoffrey had not over-
done by a syllable in what he had told me
about Quartz; the sailing *was* perfection.
Both he and Murray rallied me upon my
ravings; I seldom excite myself over scen-
ery, but am dumbest when I enjoy most.
This was so exhilarating, however, that it
made me boisterous, this swift open-sea
sailing. But if going out was lovely, coming back was lovelier; and we had every
variety of speed in our motion. The sun
was setting behind the old town, with its
irregular picturesque profile clear cut and
sharply defined against a yellow sky. We
were becalmed outside, and had a long

opportunity of observing this grand and gloomy outline, until the background was no longer yellow, and the profile ceased to be. Then the breeze freshened into a small gale; and we came spinning into the harbor, with a reefed mainsail. Geoffrey was quiet while we were out. He was either lying flat on his back, looking up at the sky, wearing a tranquil expression, — so different from the old bored look! — or he was making marks on small pieces of paper which he pulled out of his pocket.

" Let's see your sketch, old man," I said once, holding out my hand.

"It's not a sketch," he replied. " I was correcting an exercise ; I am teaching old Iron's grandchild German."

" The deuce you are!" cried Murray. " Then that's why you two are poring over books so eternally. She ferries him over, Farley, and ferries him back, and round the lighthouse, and into that little inlet over there; and they sit and chat and scribble by the hour. I hope you don't pay her by the job, Geoff ; the Iron family will soon be paupers, if you do! I thought she was trying to convert you ; and was preaching sermons to you, or writing them, rather. I did indeed. You know this little antiquated town of ours boasts a very advanced church, Farley."

"Advanced !" laughed Geoffrey. " Hear the unenlightened ; the poor Protestant ! 'T is a restoration of the original fabric, my child. Let me bring Father Worthing over to talk you into it, and not a doubt will remain. Mine have been swept away like cobwebs."

" You 'd better not let Alice hear you make light of the subject, that 's all. She 's the fiercest little churchwoman," Murray said, turning to me. " But she knows what she 's talking about, and that 's more than you do, you hardened old pagan ! " —This last to Geoff.

When we picked up our moorings, it was dark. Murray said dinner would be waiting. " It always is waiting," he said, with a sigh. " I never do get home on time, and Laura is an abused woman."

As we came up to the float, in the tender, I made out a small dory, with a girlish figure on one of the thwarts. I knew instantly, from Geoffrey's alert manner, who it was.

At the sound of our oars, the figure turned; and in the red glare of the lantern which hung high over the float, I saw a face. I knew then how Geoffrey felt. She was entrancing, bewildering! Murray had said nothing about her; Geoffrey not half enough. I was conscious of burning eyes, and a smile that would have reduced the heart of a stoic to atoms. Not for me, of course, that smile; it began at Murray, but lingered, and turned to glory when it fell on Geoff. He gave her a tender, melting glance; the two understood — or misunderstood — each other, evidently. He spoke simply to her, as we passed, fending her boat with his hand. "We had a good sail," he said.

"I saw you," responded the girl, in a fresh, sweet voice; young and yet well-modulated, like a gentlewoman's.

"I am waiting for a passenger who has gone to the Club-house," she explained, looking up at the shore. Geoffrey's face changed at once. "Row home, Alexia," he said softly, "and our man here will take the passenger over, may n't he, Murray?"

"Of course," Murray replied.

"It's much too late," continued Geoffrey, in a fatherly tone, "for you to be ferrying strangers across, my child; you must not do it!"

"But I know this gentleman," she pleaded, with a deprecatory look at Geoffrey, as if she were in the habit of obeying him. "It's Mr. Gray; a friend of yours too, Mr. Trevor," she added, turning to Murray.

"Oh, that's all right, then," said Murray, carelessly. "But it's quite true what Mr. Geoffrey says, Alice; and your grandfather must be well overhauled for sending you out alone after dark. Tell him I say so too. Good-night. Be careful." And we started up the road — the short cut — rather than along the bank, as showing more signs of "decent haste," Murray said.

Geoffrey started with us, but went back, after taking a dozen steps. "I'm going over to the Head for a few minutes," he said; "I won't be long; but don't wait dinner for me."

"You'll be awfully late, Geoff," shouted Murray; but there was no answer, and we heard the scraping of oars.

"It's all nonsense," declared Murray, "his going over now. I'll bet a hat it's only to watch that child; he's always holding forth on the subject of her being out after dark in the dory. And she is too pretty by a long sight. What do you think of her, Farley?" he said, turning to me. "Isn't she the loveliest thing you ever saw?"

"I never have seen such a face in my life," I answered shortly. Somehow, I didn't want to talk about her then. She was far above any ideal I had formed of her — or of anybody.

Was Murray — was his wife — were they all — stark, staring blind?

IV.

MRS. MURRAY TREVOR had been a dashing girl in society a few years before; she was much changed, and looked white and languid. She asked Murray to ring for dinner, as he passed through the house.to the veranda, where she was sitting.

"Murray is used to spoiled food, Mr. Farley," she said, smiling, and putting out her hand, "and so must you learn to be, if you copy his habits. But I am very glad indeed to see you, if I do begin with a scolding."

"Poor thing!" murmured Murray, stooping over her to kiss her, "why don't you have your dinner at the proper time, and leave us miserable sinners to go without, or get scrapings? It would serve us right, when we 're an hour late, — an hour and a half, by Jove!" he exclaimed, glancing at the clock through the window.

"Oh, I have no appetite when I am alone," said Laura. "Do run and get ready. I'm positively afraid to meet the cook!

"Pardon me, if I revert to this unpleasing topic of *time*," said Laura, sending away her soup, "but may I ask what men do with their watches, when they depart for what they are always pleased to call a 'little sail'? Do time-pieces stop in that enchanted region the deck of a yacht, or what is the reason that nobody ever comes home to dinner, within three hours or so of the hour set?"

"You forget, Laura," said Murray, with an aggravating air of imparting information, "that we depend upon the *wind* in sailing. If we went and came on our own feet it would be different; there would be no excuse for us then. You know I always say to you before I start, 'Don't expect me back until you see me, and have your dinner at the usual time.'"

"Yes, but I say something too," laughed Laura. "I say that when I marry a man, and he plants me on a desert island, — even if that island does afterward turn into a peninsula, — I say I like to eat one meal a day in his company, or in somebody's company. That's what *I* say."

"How did your island turn into a peninsula?" I asked Mrs. Trevor.

"Why, you know there is only a strip of sand and shingle connecting us with the mainland? Well, that used not to exist; that is to say, it has been formed gradually by storms, which threw up quantities of stones. With some help of man there has been formed a dusty and hot and windy, but nevertheless grateful, passage across. I never get into a boat, if I can help it; and it is such a comfort to know that, in case of emergency, I can pass over dry-shod to my country and my country's people."

"You are not fond of sailing, then?" I have rarely seen a yachtsman's wife who was.

"Well, I used to sail, — was quite a skipper myself, in fact, if you can believe it. I am not like the woman who told me once (her husband being a great sailor) that she could tell the difference between a sloop and a schooner only by remembering that sloop had one syllable and one mast, and schooner two! But my boating days are over now, and I am selfishly losing my interest in it."

I wondered why she lived there, so lonely and apparently so discontent. Murray Trevor was not the man to make a woman live where she did n't choose; and I have yet to be presented to the person of that gender, of any spirit, who will stay there!

" You are not specially attached to this place, then?" I said, rather stupidly.

" Yes, she is," said Murray, hastily ;. " don't mind her. Laura likes it very much, and the air agrees with her wonderfully. That's why we stay here," he added, looking affectionately at her through his eye-glass. " But, strange to say, with Laura's touch of invalidism [she had not had a well moment for three years!] she has taken a dislike to the water, — sailing, rowing, and all that ; and has even a kind of fright about it. We used to sail together constantly ; in fact, it was on Laura's account we came here originally, and it was she who made me build this house. I am awfully sorry to say she is lonely here, and utterly refuses to let any women come and stay with her."

"Oh, well, if women would come by themselves, and be contented here," said Laura; "but I seem to know only butter-flies, who either bring a lot of men with them, or look bored to death all the time. And I am not strong enough to entertain a party. I never shall forget Helen's yawns," she said, turning to Geoffrey, who had come in not long before, "when she came to spend a week with me here, once! There's nothing to do really, you know," turning to me, "except to sail; there's ab-solutely no driving, and I will not ask any-body here to mope."

"If a *well* woman mopes in this place, she's a fool!" exclaimed Murray. "I don't care whether she's engaged to you or not, Geoff."

Geoffrey paid no attention to this shaft, and I doubt if he had been listening. He spoke suddenly. "Murray, old Iron is in a way your own man; can't you make a contract with him to do your ferrying, and nobody else's?"

"I do make a contract with him," replied Murray. "He works for hardly any-body but me. But if you mean, can't I make a contract with him by which *Alice* shall row nobody else, why, I don't see how I can, exactly, Geoff. We have half-a-dozen boats of our own, now, and boys and men lying about, doing nothing, when we don't 'sail; and there is n't work enough for that stupid old donkey, Iron, as it is. The girl likes to feel she is help-ing her grandfather, and the exercise is good for her. I can tell old Iron to do his own work *at night;* for I agree with you that it's a bad thing for Alice to be out late, carrying yachtsmen across the harbor."

We had adjourned to the veranda now, while Murray was talking, and were sitting there, with our coffee. The lights in the harbor were twinkling, and those on the op-posite shore; and over on Blynn's wharf a great red eye glowed. We could hear the plashing of oars, as the poets say, and the curfew bell on Quartz Head. Otherwise it was still as death, until Mrs. Trevor spoke.

"It's a bad thing," she said, in answer to Murray's last speech, "for a girl in

Alice's position to be so pretty,— a very bad thing indeed!" This with great emphasis. "But I don't see what we can do about it. The Sisters over there, with the best and most mistaken intentions in the world, have given her a careful and admirable training — for anything but the life she leads. However, they have made her a religious, modest girl. She will have to be out at night sometimes, — all girls in her station do,—and certainly our shielding her fitfully from an occasional discomfort will only do her harm. She is very fortunate in many things," Laura added, turning to me. "They are fearfully poor, and many girls so placed would be forced to stay in a hot kitchen [Geoffrey got up from his chair, with a kind of bounce, and threw his cigar into the grass], cooking and washing and doing every kind of hard work [he was pacing the veranda now, near us], whereas she has air, exercise, and a good deal of leisure. She has been taught music, French, and the most exquisite needlework. She could earn her living by her altar-embroidery, I should think ; it is wonderful. I am sorry for

her, but in a different way from you men.
She is in an entirely false position, and
must feel it. She has had petting and
admiration enough this summer alone, to
turn twenty heads."

"Is her head turned?" I asked innocently.

"No," said Geoffrey abruptly, stopping
in his walk.

"Yes," said Laura. "I beg your pardon, Geoffrey. In the way you mean, no.
That is to say, she is neither vain nor silly.
But she knows she is not one of the same
lot as the rest over there, — her own people. You can see that, by talking with
her for two minutes, in spite of her perfectly respectful manner."

"I beg leave to differ," growled Geoffrey.

"It is patent, at least to me ; again I
beg your pardon, Geoffrey. I don't mean
to say that she makes the townspeople
feel it. She only realizes it herself, and
is too sweet, naturally, to let it be seen,
for fear it might hurt them. Her birth
is obscure, — unknown, I may say, — and
darkened by disgrace. This sounds hard
and unfeeling in me, you think, but it is
neither. I am a better friend to this poor

girl, you will find, than those who try to raise her above her life, — temporarily, and about six inches, — if it is raising her at all, which I doubt," she went on, glancing at Geoffrey, "and who will let her drop again, discontented with her lot, and worse off than ever!"

Well, Laura's trumpet gave forth no uncertain sound now! Murray had not heard any of this last, — he had gone in to get another cigar, — but Geoffrey was furious. He was silent; but his back was a study.

Laura leaned back in her chair, exhausted. She had evidently been waiting her opportunity, and had nerved herself to give Geoff this "piece of her mind." The subject dropped, and was not renewed — then.

Murray and Geoffrey strolled down to the Club or the float with their cigars, but I stayed with Mrs. Trevor. As soon as the two men had disappeared she began, as I knew she would. "You are Geoffrey's best friend and only confidant, he tells me. May I ask you what you think of his engagement?"

I hesitated. There was much to say, and
Helen Courtice was her cousin. " I think
a good deal ' of ' it, in the sense of ' about '
it," I answered, half smiling. " Geoffrey's
affairs, for some reason or other, are more
mine than my own ; I might almost say,
than his !" Then I told her how troubled
I had been at first, the engagement had
been so precipitate ; then that I had become
reconciled, seeing Geoffrey growing calm
and content ; how exasperated I had been
at Helen's going away, when matters were
running so smoothly ; and — I stopped.
I was not asked anything farther.

" H'm ; I did n't know much about this,"
said Laura, musing. " It seemed a fitting
enough match to me. Then Geoffrey has
behaved well ; and Helen, true to her
character, has been thoroughly selfish.
But do you know," she raised herself in
her chair, and looked me full in the face,
" have you any idea, what he is doing now
— down here ? "

I mumbled, in an indistinct tone, as if
I had been guilty of something, that I —
no — that is to say, I did have an idea,
but I did n't know.

"He has been here a month," began Laura, shutting her eyes, and laying her head back, as if she were very weary. "You know he came in the first place at my request. I heard he was moping, and I knew he was queer, and had no ties, so I was anxious to have him here, and to do something for him; cheer him up, if possible. He does n't like me; but I pretend not to know it, and I dare say he does n't know it himself. I have urged him to stay on with us, and so has Murray. I am not about much, nor 'in' things, and poor dear old Murray is as blind as a bat, so we have both thoroughly misunderstood the situation. This girl's beauty took hold of him at once; it is of an extraordinary kind; you have perhaps seen her? She is apt to be about with her boat."

I said yes, I had seen her; she was marvellous. If Laura knew how her face had haunted me!

"She is, truly. I tremble every time I see her; for sooner or later she is sure to be begged, borrowed, or stolen for an artist's model. The seclusion of this spot and the Sisters' care have been her salvation, so far. Geoffrey got interested in her studies first, and talked all the time about her pluck and her intelligence. He is twice her age, and I thought nothing about it, except to be glad that she had such a patron, and he such an interest. Then he began to pity her, and to do little things to make her life brighter. He sent her a dress, which the Sisters declined for her, however [Oho! Mr. Geoff]; he arranged her time, so that she could be with him constantly; he brought her books, and he taught her German. Latterly he is with her morning, noon, and night, and naturally the girl chafes at any duty which keeps her away from him. I am sure this is the first afternoon he has given to Murray for a fortnight, and he rarely sits an hour after dinner with him or me. They row about usually, I believe, he and Alice. It's perfectly dreadful, and I feel as if I somehow were very much to blame about it."

"Has Geoffrey told you all this?" I asked, in amazement. It was very unlike him to speak of it to her.

"Oh dear, no!" Her lip curled. "Not

a word.   And if you will believe so absurd
a statement, I have never even suspected
this until to-day.   Sister Ignatia, a sweet,
charming little Englishwoman, came here
this morning, and poured out her woes to
me.   She is worried to death; they res-
cued Alice from the gutter, one might almost say, — for the babies of such people
play where their fathers fall ; and she has
endeared herself to them by her lovely,
docile ways, and by her affection, too.
They have authority over Alice, and yet
they have n't ; she is free to go and come,
and her work is with her oars, you know.
I could see the Sister but a few minutes,
for I was keeping the doctor waiting, but
we are to have another interview."

"Does this girl know that Geoffrey is
engaged, do you suppose ?"

" I don't know.   I suppose so.   At least
I did, if I supposed anything.   I can't tell.
You see I have n't known ; I have n't had
time to suppose.   I should say there was
as great a probability that she did, as that
she did n't.   She does n't know yet that
she loves him, as I take it, and won't until he leaves her.   It 's this horrible awak-

ening, at the wrenching asunder, that I dread for the child. It will kill her; she has an intense nature, Sister Ignatia says."

It was a hard case. "Geoffrey 's not a deceiver," I said, "I mean a wilful one. He 's a fearful blunderer, and I doubt if he has the remotest idea of what he is doing. He was angry with you to-night, not because of what you said, so much, as that you were trying to thwart him. He has always had his own way."

"Well, I *am* thwarting the gentleman from this moment," she said grimly. "Somebody must do it, and at once."

I said I recognized the truth of that statement, and would help her.

"Well," she said, "what 's the first thing to do ?"

"Tell the girl distinctly that he is going to be married."

"But suppose she knows it ?"

"Tell her that Geoffrey is injuring her forever."

"You don't understand girls, I see. She would constitute herself his champion, deny the charge, defy us, and quarrel

with the whole town for his sake. Try
again."

"Tell her he's injuring the other girl."

"Ah! that's better ; or best of all, that
he is ruining *himself!* That will do it.
Poor little thing! Don't you pity her?"

Pity her! Every time I thought of
those great, glorious eyes, turning full upon that miscreant Geoffrey, with the love
she herself knew not, glowing in them
and out of them; and of that heavenly
smile, frank and unfearing, I had seen her
bestow upon the scamp, I felt as if an
assassin were a cooing dove to me, plot-
ting her misery. Yet misery it was for
her, poor lamb, on either path, and it
might better be unaccompanied, or un-
caused, by *her* misdoing. Dear little
thing! How different I felt, now that I
had seen her! Geoffrey might have raved
about her in four languages; one look did
more for me than all his apostrophes.

"I have a plan, I think," said Laura,
after a pause. "Don't let Geoffrey see
her much to-morrow, if you can help it;
and by Monday I shall have arranged to
keep them apart. Will you kindly ring

for my maid? I am very tired!" And
she was, — worn out.

Laura had hardly gone, when I heard
the two men coming up the steps outside.
I felt like a felon, — a plotter always does,
no matter how much in the right he may
be, when he meets the object of his machi-
nations. "Where have you been, you
two?" I asked sleepily, although I never
was wider awake in my life. First down-
ward step of a conspirator!

"Oh, I went to see a sail-maker about
a new jib," Murray rejoined, "and Geoff
has been hanging about Blynn's, buzzing
the fishermen, have n't you, Geoff?"

"Then you 've been over to the town?"
I asked, suspicion seizing me. He was
not so fascinated with fishermen that he
spent whole evenings with them, I knew!

"Yes," yawned, or rather growled,
Geoffrey. He had not recovered his
good-nature, it seemed, since Laura's attack, or else the sight of me revived it.
"I 'll go to bed, I think. Good-night, old
man. Good-night, Murray."

After Geoffrey's footsteps had died away
on the stair, and we heard him stumping

about overhead, Murray spoke. " Geoff 's
all up a tree to-night," he said ; " got
bad news, — a despatch from Helen at
Homburg."

" What ! " I gasped. She might have
thrown him over. Oh, joy ! if she only
had !

" It was sent down from town to Quartz.
Her mother has died suddenly, and she
sailed from Bremen to-day ! "

By Jove !

V.

I WONDER if Geoffrey passed half as sleepless a night as I did that Saturday. I hope so, I'm sure. I don't mind lying awake for his sins, if he does it too ; but to do all the tossing and turning, and never to have had any of the fun, seems an unequal division. It poured toward morning, and I fell asleep, and such a curious spectacle as I woke to find! It was half foggy, half bright, and the sun burning its way, in luminous patches, through the mist, made lovely, mirage-like pictures, which shifted every moment. When I looked out first the tops of one or two very high buildings on the shore, and the bottoms of the boats — of course I mean the lowest parts above water — only were to be seen. That is to say, a broad belt of vapor hid all the rest. The belt was adjustable ; for soon the lower houses and the middle green appeared. Now and

then a topsail would shine out spectrally
from a bank of fog, or perhaps a bright-
colored pennant, or a golden ball. These
wraith-like, delicate effects changed constantly, and it was a magic hour I spent,
watching them.

Geoffrey came down after we had finished breakfast and were lounging about,
a little limp from the dampness. He
handed me the telegram he had received
the night before.

"Trevor told me," I said, as I handed it
back, after reading it. "It's awful. What
a frightful ending to the summer's pleasure!
Who is with Miss Courtice, Geoffrey?"

"The Leonards and Lorimers," he replied, "and some English people the Cour-
tices have known for years. Everybody
will be kind, of course; but it is horrible,
as you say. Poor Helen! I'm afraid she
will be ill."

"They never should have carted the
poor old lady over there at her time of
life," remarked Murray, who was perched
on the veranda-railing, cutting off the
end of a cheroot. "The last voyage I took
with her I thought they would never get

her home. Helen Courtice will kill all
her relations, dragging them off to Europe.
It's a mania with her. She's a perfect
wandering Jew. Don't you let her hawk
you about the continent, Geoff; she'll kill
you, as sure as she does!"

"Murray," exclaimed Laura, who had
just appeared for a moment, at the door,
"your delicacy is truly infinite. Now,.
Geoffrey, as your cousin's wife, and your
wife's cousin, I am qualified to advise you.
Marry Helen the minute she gets home,
and settle down in this country. It's a—"

"My very dear respected cousin's wife,
and prospective wife's cousin," interrupted.
Geoffrey, rudely,—he was still angry with
Laura,— "I never took advice from a living soul yet, and neither did Helen, not
even from each other; so I doubt if we
begin now. But thank you all the same."

"Well, Geoffy," said Murray, hopping
down, and slapping him on the back, "if
you won't be married the instant Helen
lands, and before she's buried her mother,
you will have some breakfast now, won't
you?" And they went through the doorway together, into the dining-room.

Laura was sitting at a long window in the drawing-room, and I was near her, in the veranda. An old bent, sunburned fellow was seen clambering up the bank, from the water's edge. He looked a kind of Sinbad, with his shaggy white eyebrows and long white beard, or perhaps more like a sea-faring Santa Claus. He had gold hoops in his ears, and wore a blue and white checked calico "jumper." He took off his battered straw hat, I thought at first as a salutation, but it was only to wipe his forehead, I found; and he replaced it before coming into Mrs. Trevor's presence. He hitched along toward us, and backing up against the veranda railpost, lounged, or shuffled, there.

"Good-mornin'," he said casually. "No sailin' this mornin', I guess. I come up on an arrant," he said, his lips smacking between every two phrases, so that I at once recognized Geoffrey's portrait of him. "This mornin' my Alice was out with the green dory." He addressed himself impartially to Mrs. Trevor and me; looking first at one, and then the other. "'Alice,' I says to her, 'where be you a-goin' with

that dory?' You see it wa'n't but six
o'clock. 'Gran'father,' she says, 'wal,'
she says, 'I'm a-goin' to row Mr. Geoffery
Tree-vor over to church, an' that's where
I'm a-goin',' she says."

Mrs. Trevor and I exchanged despair-
ing glances. It was evident we had got to
get up early in the morning to circumvent
Mr. Geoff!

"You see, sir," he explained, turning to
me, " they's a little church over there, and
my Alice she goes reg'lar."

Geoffrey appeared at the dining-room
door. " Oh, you're there, Iron, are you?
And you found my sleeve-button in the
dory too," he added, seeing a glistening
object in the old man's hand. " I'm much
obliged to you ;" and he held out a coin.

"No," said the old man, emphatically,
drawing back, and eying the money with
a greedy look. " *No*, sir ; you've done me
an' the child too many good turns for us
to take your quarters of dollars, — or is it
a half?" he inquired, trying to get a good
look at it.

Geoffrey put it into his hand.

"You're determint on givin' it to me,

aint you, sir, an' it's a whole dollar too,"
he chuckled.

"Look you, Iron," said Murray, strolling out. He was always a day after the fair, and had heard nothing. "Don't you let that pretty girl of yours go out rowing after dark alone; do you hear me? You ought to be ashamed of yourself. With all the money I pay you, and Mr. Geoffrey here pays you, you can't be so hard up for fifteen cents that you have to send that young thing out at night, you grasping old duffer! You don't deserve to have her at all."

Old Iron grinned, displaying dental deficiencies by the dozen. "I'm a-goin' to tell you all about that, Mr. Tree-vor; you see, Alice she got kint o' anxious about me, 'cause I was out a-fishin', an' it come on to blow. So the gal started out in the green dory; and while she was a kint o' scootin' round, lookin' for me, — 't wa'n't really blowin', you know, only it looked kint o' black, — wal, a gentleman he come, a-callin', on the wharf, an' says he, kint o' mad, 'Where's all the ferrymen?' says he. 'I can't see nobody to row me over. What do I pay for reg'lar,' says he, 'an' all the men gone?' Jest then he see Alice, who was a-comin' up, an' he says, 'You come an' row me acrost, my dear,' says he, 'an' you come reg'lar,' says he, 'for me;' an' then he says to Blynn, who was jest a-comin' down on the wharf, 'This's the gal for me,' he says, 'an' will cut you loafers all out,' he says, 'gettin' the business away from you. We like to go over with sech a beauty,' he says, a-winkin' to Blynn. So, then, when Alice she gets over to the float, 'You wait for me,' he says to her, 'an' carry me back.' It wa'n't dark then, but he kep' her a-waitin' half a nour, an' thet's how it come to be dark when you see her a-settin' there."

Geoffrey had gnawed his lip and nervously thrummed with his foot while this yarn was in progress, and his face had grown blacker and blacker. He knew enough not to "let fly," however, and it was Murray who spoke.

"You'd better keep that girl close, now I tell you, Iron," he said seriously, "and that's my advice to you. It won't do her any good to hear things like that, and if she's got to be kept waiting in the dark, as she was last night, we'll see that she goes back to the 'Sisters,' and stays there. But I'll tell you what I'll do, old man. I'll make you a new business offer, and we will go down on the rocks and talk it over." So they went off down the bank together, the old man looking as if he would break his neck at every step, or plunge.

Geoffrey pretended to read the paper.

"There's one difficulty disposed of," I said, drawing my chair near him, and sitting down, "but not the biggest one."

"What in thunder do you mean?" snarled Geoffrey.

"I mean that *you* are the biggest difficulty that poor girl has to contend against. Do you understand me now? Can't you see how you are hurting her?"

"No," he retorted angrily, "I can't; but I *can* see how you and Laura and that infernal old idiot, her grandfather, are trying hard to do it!" And he got up from his chair in a rage, and went off.

I was wild to see the girl again, and by daylight; not from curiosity, I thought,

so much as to find out the best way of
helping her. So I strolled down to the
float-stage, and, oddly enough, Alice was
just bringing her boat up alongside, with
one of the Trevors' servant-maids, coming
from church, as passenger.

"Can you row me across?" I asked.

She looked up brightly, but never smiled,
as she had smiled on Geoff. "I can't for
ten minutes or so, sir," she replied. "I'm
sorry; but I'm waiting for my grandfather,
who has gone up to the house. [The Trevors' was "the house" to all the townspeople.] He has to be back over there,"
pointing to the town, "at twelve; but
one of Blynn's men will take you, sir,"
she added, as another dory appeared out
of the mist.

"No, no," I hastened to object, "I can
wait perfectly well; I have nothing special
to hurry me."

She was holding the boat with a little
brown hand.

"Shall I get in?" I asked.

"If you please, sir."

So I got into the stern, and gazed at
her, for she hardly looked at me. Pretty!

Well, she was exquisite; a thousand times more beautiful by day than she had been by the crimson glare of the lantern. It was the kind of beauty that sunlight brings out, and touches up, and intensifies. I could no more do her justice with this poor pen than I could catch the changing hues of the last night's sunset with a camera. Yet no detail was lost upon me. It was a childish face, and yet a womanly. Great masses of gleaming hair, dark in the shade, bronze in the light, framed it. I had not even noticed her beautiful hair the night before; she was a queen without that, but now that her eyes and her smile were not prejudicing my judgment, it seemed her chief glory. Her face was serene in repose, and full of dignity; spirited in action, and teeming with vivacity. When she spoke or smiled, everything spoke and smiled too, — her eyes danced, her white teeth flashed, her dimples and her blushes played, and little fascinating pink changes came and went in her chin. I had not seen her angry; but she could be that too, I knew. It was a face that would be grand in storms.

I was completely staggered by her loveliness ; I own it.

The patronizing little speeches which I had cut and dried, on my way from the house, stuck in my throat, in the presence of this queenly innocent. Her movements were marked with easy grace. The dingy gown was shapeless, and patched and darned ; but a lithe figure made itself known through the disguise. A crimson handkerchief — Geoffrey's gift — was knotted loosely about the whitest of rounded throats. Flaw there was none, as Geoffrey had said. She was pluperfect!

The old man kept us waiting a long time ; and Alice, who had taken out a book, glanced now and then uneasily in the direction of the Trevors'. Perhaps she had an appointment with Geoffrey, my wicked thought suggested. It might be embarrassing for her, my sitting directly opposite her so long, it occurred to me, so I got out of the boat, walked about a bit, then came back, and sat on one of the steps of the float, holding the gunwale with my foot. At last I managed to say, as her eyes were not upon me, "You are not fit for this sort of work."

She looked up, astonished. "Why?" she asked simply, her glorious deep-gray eyes, with their heavy fringes, full of wonder.

"You are too young," I answered, not as bold as I had been. What eyes, what eyes!

"I am seventeen," she said, "and very strong; and even little children row. I can pull for hours without feeling it. I never tire myself. And this dory is small and light. So are my oars. Look!" And she held up a graceful spoon-oar of spruce. "Mr. Geoffrey Trevor gave Grandfather these." She smiled, saying this.

"You are too pretty," I dared to say, giving another of my reasons. She looked up, astonished, again, and something else, —angry, I thought. She replied with grave dignity this time. The smile was miles away.

"I am well known here, sir," she said, in a low tone, but with a heightened color, "and I am very good at looking after myself. This is my own work, which I try to mind quietly."

"My own business," she might have said, but she was perhaps more considerate of my feelings than I had been of hers. I could hear the sound of tears in her low voice; she was pulling out the row-locks nervously, and putting them in again, and I could not see her eyes.

As she sat discomposed, disturbed, even alarmed or angry, — for I could not read her mind just then, — so beautiful in her agitation, so utterly, totally out of keeping with her fate, I felt the justice of Laura's remarks more keenly than ever. If this sensitive, sweet creature was not aware of her superiority over the townspeople, — her own people, as Laura had truly named them, — she was wanting in everything she disclosed, — a moral paradox she must be.

I was not proud of myself. I might have known my brutal method would be the very worst and most unsuccessful one. I had done well! — made her cry the first thing, and ranked myself among her enemies. She changed her position, and threw off her discomfiture like magic.

"Have you been here much, sir?" she

said. "We have such good fishing just outside; only my grandfather says there is a fashion in fishing, and it has gone by just now." She was trying to be professional, and her air was very business-like. "We used to let our dories too a good deal; but everything now is sailing —just for the love of it. That is Mr. Grant's cutter over there, the Godiva; it has only six feet of beam. But there is still a smaller one, the Shiva; it holds only one man at a time, — four feet across, I think, it is. Pretty narrow, I call that." And she laughed a forced little laugh, and prattled on. I was not to have another opportunity of airing my views, it seemed. It was a clever little woman, then. Perhaps the cornered mouse will show fight. I never observed one.

"Blynn is going to have a steam-ferry," she announced. "Then our business will be gone, I suppose, unless Grandfather can get a position on it. He is growing old very fast, I can see it; and he loses his breath, and his eyes are not good. It is very sad to grow old." A safe general statement.

"Then, when Blynn's steam-ferry takes away your work, what will *you* do ?" I said. I seemed to be saying the most brutal things to this girl ; what was the matter with me ? I had not thought how that would sound !

"Oh," she responded gayly, " I shall do other work. The Sisters say I can be sure of money enough; they have taught me a good many things."

"Mr. Trevor says you are learning German."

She flushed, and a most unmistakable joy glanced from her eyes and played about her lips. She smiled. "I am stupid about it, *I* think. [Then he did n't?] Sometimes I make very bad blunders. But oh, how I like it!" She looked at me, and said, drawing a deep breath, "Have you ever read 'Undine'? Mr. Geoffrey and I are translating it together."

I nodded.

"Is n't it a most beautiful story? There is one place I tried three times to read aloud, and could n't, the tears choked me so! It reminds me of a book I was reading aloud to the Sisters once, when I was

small. It is called 'At the Back of the
North Wind.' When I came to the last
chapter I cleared my voice, and coughed,
and pretended to have a cold. And at last
I laid the book down, put my head on my
arms on the table, and cried it out! The
Sisters often remind me of that. They
never cry, I think."

"Perhaps they do in secret," I suggested. "Are n't they very unhappy?"

"Oh, *unhappy!*" almost shouted Alice,
roused entirely out of herself, and looking
unspeakably lovely. "*No!* They are perfectly happy, and because they are good.
They are tempted constantly; both these
Sisters here have naturally strong wills
and quick tempers, and each of them
often thinks her way the best. But they
conquer themselves; and they are so meek
and so patient after it! And *oh*, how
hard they work! Everybody in Quartz
Head, *every single body*" (she used quaint
little terms now and then, like a child) "is
better for their living in the town. I could
not begin to tell you of the good they do.
They are as near following our Blessed
Lord's example as any of the saints. And

they would be martyrs too, in a minute, if the chance came to them."

She seemed to feel at home with me now and was talking naturally.

"And do the Sisters quite approve of your doing this work, — this ferrying ?" I asked tentatively.

She shrank up again. "They do," she answered, with sweet dignity, but far from me, "or I should not be doing it."

I had no answer by me at the moment; I might have thought of twenty, away from those eyes !

Old Iron came hitching along, while I was thus embarrassed, and began to talk, of course, as soon as he hove in sight. "You need n't a waited ef you had a passenger," he shouted, in his cracked voice. "I was a-talkin' with Mr. Tree-vor ; him an' me has a good deal o' business to talk together." He shambled into the dory, and took a pair of oars. "You see," he went on, as he thumped them into the row-locks, and prepared to pull, — "you see, Alice, — wal, we 've got a new kint of arrangement now; you aint to be out any more o' nights, an' I aint sure as I shall let you — "

"Grandfather!" cried Alice, imploringly, "will you be quiet about my affairs? Don't you see there's a strange gentleman with us? It's no worse my doing my own work [how she clung to that adjective!] late, than your talking me over like this with everybody!" There was no doubt about the tears now. They choked her speech.

The old man was evidently overwhelmed with surprise. "Alice!" he said severely, "you go on with your rowin', an' don't you never let me hear sech talk agin. This gentleman is a rintimate friend of Mr. Tree-vor's and Mr. Geoffery's both, an' I jest seen him up to the house, a-settin' with 'em, on the — the, — *with 'em*," he added, the word being too much for him, or escaping him. "I would n't talk you over with non' but friends, Alice, an' I could n't say nothin' but good of you," he whimpered, sliding rapidly down from his very temporary perch, and looking abjectly at Alice, who was still displeased, and showed it. "But this I will say, that when ladies an' gentlemen like the Tree-vor family takes an interest in us, we 'd oughter let 'em jedge what's best for our good."

Poor Alice! It was impossible to believe that this garrulous, tough-skinned, mercenary old imbecile had the same blood in his veins which coursed in hers.

I tried to apologize to her in a low tone, very lamely, I know, for what I had said.

" It's nothing, sir," she said, with a kind of sad smile; and I longed to apologize again. " I should learn to take advice; but Grandfather blurts out everything to everybody, and then I did think, honestly, sir, that you were a little outspoken, when you know nothing about me. [Nothing! Good gracious! As if her affairs had not been the principal topic of conversation ever since I had come there!] I beg your pardon, sir." Her cheeks were blazing, her sweet lips tremulous, and her eyes glowing like coals; and of course she was more entrancingly lovely than ever!

The row is a short one; it seemed like nothing, it was so soon over. Mr. Geoff was lounging on the pier, smoking; I saw a small Whitehall boat bobbing against the piles, and I knew how he had got there. He glanced at me, blew out a cloud of smoke, threw away his cigar, approached Alice, and asked her where she was going. " Home," she said. She lifted her face to him, with a joyous look in it like a happy child's. " I'll go up the hill with you; may I?" This was a bold stroke. My morning's work had not been madly successful, so far. But as I saw that infernal old nuisance, Iron, hobbling after the pair, and marked that Geoffrey dismissed himself at the corner, I felt better. He had n't made much by that move!

Laura told me in the afternoon that she had sent word to the Sisters that she would provide sewing for Alice, so that the child might be kept in-doors for the present. Poor Laura was exhausted, for she could bear almost nothing, and I did n't see her again during that little visit.

VI.

LATE in the day Geoffrey thought there might be another despatch for him at Quartz, so I accompanied him over to see, and Alice rowed us back, or at least offered to do so. Geoffrey told her to sit still, and he would do the rowing. I knew what an effort it cost him not to oust me from the stern and put her tenderly there, and make her comfortable with his coat. Oh, it was useless to argue the point of her birth, or her degree. She was as gently turned out as the finest lady in the land, and no more appropriately set where she was than a jewel in a swine's snout. It was absurd to disguise the fact, and we both treated her with as much deference as we dared.

There was a magnificent sky of liquid gold, and we made out another sea and villages and trees, and even people, in it. Alice was in a gay, bantering mood, and

Geoffrey caught it from her. She was
confiding and coquettish with him, and altogether fascinating. He looked at her
all the time. So did I. Who could blame
either of us?

Alice sat upon the thwart, her oars lying idly by, and her hands folded in her
lap. That she was serenely happy at being in the presence of Geoffrey, and that
there had been no change in his attitude
toward her, was plain. Her manner
toward him was artless and joyful, as, I
suppose, it had always been. It gave me
a kind of guilty pleasure to see those two
attractive and uncommon beings together.
Alice hardly ever spoke first, and when
she did, it was with a little touch of deference and coquetry impossible to describe,
and bewitching to witness.

"Alexia," said Geoffrey, — and he made
her name a caress, — "that parson does n't
speak loud enough in the what d' you call
it, — mass? — the mass. I could n't hear
half he said. And what's the name of
that superb circular he wears? And
where did he get it? And why does he
wear it?"

"Oh, what a lot of silly questions!" exclaimed Alice, glancing up at him, with her head on one side, and slapping her hands to get the salt water off them. She had her hair in a great brown plait down her back, and was altogether five years younger than she had been in the morning. "I embroidered nearly the whole of that 'circular,' as you call it, myself. It's a cope, and he wears it because it's the proper vestment for festivals."

"Well, nothing can cope with it for magnificence," retorted Geoffrey, who seemed in a merry mood, for an orphan-in-law so recently bereaved. "I did n't know it was a festival, or I would have worn *my* best things too. I have some lovely embroidered shirts, and a beautiful new flowered waistcoat. I'm so sorry I have n't observed the day properly, — dressed for it, I mean. What festival is it?"

"It's Whitsunday, of course," said Alice; "a fine churchman you must be, not to know it! Did n't you hear the Gospel and the Epistle and the Collect? The clergyman was not as indistinct as all that, I'm sure! And didn't you see the red altar-cloth?"

"I did," answered Geoffrey, demurely; "I both listened and observed. But why I should infer that a red altar-cloth, and — pardon me, I am about to pun again — a read Collect, Epistle, and Gospel should denote a whit, or white, Sunday, I cannot, with lightning rapidity, comprehend."

And this was Geoffrey Trevor, who hated puns, and who particularly disapproved of a flippant tone in speaking of serious things. But that was in other people, to be sure!

"Oh dear, dear, dear!" sighed Alice, pretending to be in great distress, "and have I worked over you all these weeks for this? Don't tell anybody you are my pupil," she said imploringly. "You must know — I must have told you — that the red is for the flame, — the cloven tongues, as of fire, that came and 'sat' upon the Apostles' heads? Don't let such ignorance go any farther. I will go over the whole subject with you to-morrow, if you like, or to-night, if you are coming to Vespers."

"Oh, yes, he was coming to Vespers," Geoffrey hastened to say. Of course he was. Trust him for that. He *must* come now, he said, and learn more about the day. They did not insist upon my going, I noticed. In fact, for some time I had been quite overlooked. Well, the sewing, the ruthless, inexorable sewing was forming itself into gores and gussets — gory gussets, I had almost said — for those little hands in the morning. It might even now be undergoing the process of " basting," — an appropriate term, I thought, — and poor Alice was having her last day of peace. So was Geoffrey. For any way, and come what might, I was going to have it out with him that night. How cruel we seemed to that child ! But there are degrees of cruelty, and I knew who was inflicting the worst !

We three men dined together, and Geoffrey left for his Vespers, in the middle of the meal. Murray and I sat afterward and smoked, and I tried to arrange my plan of attack. In spite of Geoffrey's misconduct, I did so long to find a good easy way out of the difficulty for him ! I would

have married the other girl — the super-
fluous one — myself, with joy, if it had
been possible, — Helen Courtice — anybody; for if I were to try, I could never
tell the hold that fellow Geoffrey had on
me. But there could be no easy path; it
must all be very hard going now. I saw
nothing but dreariness and blackness in
the outlook. Geoff was bound to be miserable in any case now, and his duty had
become his necessity; a choice of two evils
even was denied him.

What an ass he had been, to engage
himself to Helen Courtice, in the first
place! Why should he ever have sacri-
ficed himself for her? She was nothing
to him, and would never have given up a
pin's worth of pleasure for him, — a vain,
shallow-pated thing, with only looks and
lucre, as Murray once said, to recommend
her.

Murray and I were still sitting in the
veranda when Geoffrey came in, which he
did rather early. I had sounded Murray
a little, enough to find that he cherished
the absurd fallacy yet of Geoffrey's devotion to Helen; and when I mentioned

his fancy for Alice, he pooh-poohed it as preposterous, and was even impatient with me for mentioning it. Geoff of course admired her, he said ; so did he ; so did I ; but he would n't forget himself so far as to flirt with one of his (Murray's) servants, while he was under that roof. So I let the matter drop, as far as Murray was concerned.

Geoffrey sat for a few minutes with us after he came in ; but only a few, and then he went off upstairs. After I supposed him to be in bed, I knocked at his door. He was sitting, dressed, at the window.

"May I come and smoke with you?" I asked.

"I'm not smoking," was the short reply.

"May I come and sit then ?"

"If you like," in a tone of indifference.

I sat down, at this pressing invitation. "Geoff," I said, "I've got something to say to you."

"Well, keep it," he retorted gruffly, "whatever it is, until I'm in a better mood. I'm as cross as the Devil to-night, and bothered out of my life, and I know what you are going to say," he said, with a kind of burst,. "if that will save you any trouble." His voice was hoarse and hollow.

"You should n't sit at that window, Geoff," I said, for the fog was thick in the room; "you are hoarse from it now." He did n't stir. "Oh, sit round here, can't you?" I exclaimed, "and let me say what I must say, to your face. You're not a fool nor a baby, Geoff, and you can bear to hear the truth from me."

He wheeled round quickly enough at these last words. "Oh," he shouted in wrath, hurling his unlighted cigar out of the window, and springing to his feet, "is a man never to be free from this eternal prying and sneaking and lecturing? I tell you, Felix, you are making more mischief with your ridiculous suspicions than you can ever undo! I try to help a friendless child, who is struggling on through this beastly world, with every blamed thing against her, and you, with Laura at your elbow, start up a sensational scare of my trying to steal her young affections, and all that sort of trash. And not only that, but you fill other people's heads too. Now they are going to shut the child up, thanks to your friendly offices, and make her sew all day in a stuffy room, to keep her away from me. Oh, I have discovered your scheme," — for I showed my surprise. "Of course I remove myself to-morrow, and make her think there's a great deal in it, when there's nothing. You've come down here to meddle, and you've meddled, and I hope you are pleased with yourself. Only don't ask me to hear you preach about it."

"Well, if you're going away to-morrow, that's all I want," I remarked coolly. "I don't care what you call me, nor what brought you to it. You know it's your plain duty, or you would not be forced to it so easily. You know right from wrong as well as — "

"*Will* you go to bed?" roared Geoffrey. "I swear I'll put you out of this room, if you don't go yourself!"

It was not a dignified position. I had accomplished my object, however, and could afford to sneak out, so long as victory was hidden somewhere in the folds of my trailing banner. Of course Geoffrey

was angry with me. I had surprised and
routed him.

When I was fairly outside the door, and
had closed it behind me, it opened again;
and Geoffrey, coming after me, took hold
of my arm, and dragged me in without a
word. For a moment, I thought he was
a lunatic. It was only that he had been
one, and was coming to his senses.

"I'm rough to-night, Felix," he apol-
ogized, as soon as he had got me well
inside the room, and the door was shut,
"and coarse, — a brute ; a beast ; I know
it. And a coward withal, because I know
you will never resent a word I say to you.
But you are all out in this affair, and it
enrages me to be wilfully misinterpreted.
Now listen to me."

I listened ; that is to say, I should have
listened, if he had said anything. But he
did n't. He did not look, even then, like
an injured man, suffering from false accu-
sations. He had not that aspect of honest
indignation ; quite the reverse. He leaned
against the window-frame in a dreary, de-
spairing attitude, with his face turned
away. The stillness was deathlike ; the

moon had gone behind a cloud; a wet, wringing mist filled the room; it was very dark, and the air stifling. It would have been an excellent night for Lucrezia Borgia, and one she would have chosen for her blackest deed. I felt as if I were she, and had chosen it for mine.

"Well, Geoffrey," I said at last, breaking the silence, for I believe another second of it would have strangled me. Why should he stand before me mute, if the subject was so simple, and I so mistaken?

I was puzzled by this curious dumbness on Geoffrey's part; this apparent inability to utter a sound. He had once or twice made an effort, but words would not come. And fears more horrible than I had ever entertained, and suspicions more sickening than I had ever dared harbor, flashed through my mind like swords. I beg your pardon for them here and now, Geoffrey Trevor; I knew in my heart then, as I have always known, that crime and you had not one breath in common. But runaway thoughts will trespass, and I had driven the intruders out before Geoffrey found his voice.

"Well," he muttered after at least ten minutes' silence, "what shall I say? What is there for a doomed man to say? I am fettered ; what I long to do, I cannot do ; and what I loathe to do, I must do. Of course I have known, ever since Helen left me to my gloomy thoughts, — for I told her how afraid I was of them, and begged her not to go, — that that venture was worse than vain, and that she cares nothing for me. I deserve it, I know. I have given little ; I should have expected little, or nothing, in return. I know I ought to suffer, and I can suffer. I should have gone with Helen this summer ; I shall never leave her again. I have had wild dreams of being free from her, God forgive me ! But now that she is in trouble and loneliness, poor girl, I am more than ever bound to her. But — but —" He stopped and caught his breath.

"But what, Geoffrey ? " I asked anxiously. I really did n't know. Had Alice confessed her unhappy love for him that evening ? Had he just found out the extent of the harm he had wrought her ? I asked him, framing the question so as to make it as gentle as I could.

" No, *no!* " he fairly howled. " No, no! She has said nothing — But *I,* Felix, I —"

I knew it now. "But you have found, Geoffrey, now it is too late, that *you* love *her* — that you cannot give her up. Is that it ? "

He clutched at the curtain, and trembled like a hunted animal. I could hardly hear his answer. "It is. O God! It is." And a groan broke from him.

Poor old Geoffrey! He had been deceiving himself with a vengeance! And love with him, now that it had really come, was a frenzy. And he had only just found it out himself!

"Poor old fellow!" I said soothingly, and I patted him on the back like a dog. " Poor dear old Geoff! Let 's think what can be done."

"Done!" he called out savagely, — "done! What have I 'done' already ? Spoiled the lives of two women, to say nothing of this curse of hell I call my own! That was born blasted, so I could n't have injured that. Spoiled the lives of two women," he repeated, " the one 's for time, the other 's for eternity. The damage to Helen can be repaired by matrimony," he sneered, " but the pain I have caused that precious heart, God love it! over there," and he pointed to the shadows of the sleeping town, sombre and sad in the veiled moonlight and the mist, "can never, never be assuaged. I swear to you, Felix, that I never knew it, never dreamed it, till to-night. I told her I must go away; six words brought tears, and I could not say the seventh.

"I knelt beside her in the chapel to-night; I, the black reprobate, touching the hem of her gown! And she, the purest and sweetest of angels, radiant in her own dazzling beauty, and shining with goodness beside, with the candle-light giving her unearthly brilliancy, and the incense perfuming her gleaming hair, — she, rapt in visions of heaven, prayed for me, ugly, unredeemed villain that I always must remain; prayed that I might be happy and rich and beloved, and that I might find God! This she told me after-

ward ; but strange to say, at the moment
she must have been praying for me, *it* —
the knowledge of this mighty love — came
over me, all at once, like an avalanche.
Then I knew that my hopes — hopes I
did not dream I cherished — were in the
dust ; my heart was cut into a thousand
bits ! I have never thought of love, I find,
far less known it, until now ; not a glimmer has ever brightened me ; not a breath
stirred me."

For such agony I had no word. Only,
my hopes were in the dust, with his ; *my*
heart was cut into a thousand bits too.
Oh to have borne it all for him !

"Felix," he said, coming toward me,
and speaking in a solemn whisper, " once I
was watching with my father, who was very
ill. We had had a long dreary time of it, —
nights upon nights, nights upon nights, —
waiting for him to come to conscious-
ness ; to speak to us. This night I speak
of had been as long as the rest of my life
put together, it seemed ; and while I was
wondering if it would ever end, and, jaded,
unrefreshed, was thinking how dreary and
how long life was, one of the nurses went

to the window, and gently opened a shutter. It was dawn at last; and the cool, sweet morning air stole in, and fanned and revived me; and although it did not cure my pain, I slept. That is how this dear minister of grace, this angel, came to me, — like the pure, fresh morning air, — after, not nights, but years, of weariness of soul. And I, although I had no right to the refreshment, have slept; and have let her soothe and lull me. The awakening has come, however, and the old trouble is pressing harder than before. But as the air becomes vitiated upon entering the sick-room, so I have tainted her. For although I will die before she shall dream I suspect it, she loves me, Felix."

Of course she did. "Does she know why you leave her?" I asked, as gently as I could. I hated to catechise him now.

"No. I began to tell her; I mean I said I must go away, and she sobbed. I heard her. Then, coward that I am, I dared not inflict another wound. I have tried a thousand times to tell her of my engagement to Helen, but I knew she would not understand; and I thought it might make a barrier between us; I mean to our pleasant intercourse. To-night I had a mad hope that I might break it off; the other, I mean. But now that I am away from Al — her — I see that it cannot be."

It was not an opportune moment for that, I admitted. He might, to be sure, tell Alice that he was going to end his engagement with Helen as soon as her grief had subsided sufficiently for him to do so with decency! But that would hardly pave the way for future success with Alice. It was a bad business, and I told him so. But he must be helped through it, no matter whose fault it was. And we would put our shoulders to the wheel in dead earnest! We could work together, now that he had given me his confidence.

It was such a relief to Geoffrey to throw off the mask, that he fairly revelled — if anything so grim can be called a revel — in self-reproaches, and hurled them at himself perpetually. He called himself every kind of hard name. "That I," he groaned, "*I*, who long to carry her in my arms, and save her from the grind of life, and tend her, like the lamb she is, should have done my best — my worst — to ruin her!"

"Oh no, dear Geoff," I said, "it's not as bad as that." And yet I knew it was.

"It's as bad as that, and worse than that. If she had ever seen a man — anything other than those working fellows over there, I mean — I should have stood no chance with her. But I have deliberately set to work to make myself necessary to her, only to desert her. The biggest ruffian in the world is a gentleman to me."

It was characteristic of Geoffrey that having vaulted to one extreme, in announcing himself innocent, and perhaps thinking himself so, he now plunged to the other, in declaring himself guilty of more than he had really done.

"You did *not* go into it deliberately, Geoff," I said; "why do you say that? Your first idea was simply that of befriending a poor girl, was it not?"

"Oh, of course I 'did n't mean it' at first; but that does n't improve matters a bit. I saw how beautiful and uncommon she

was at one glance, and how utterly out of
keeping with her surroundings. But I did
know, if I knew anything, that a man like
me could n't better a girl like her, by hanging about her all day trying to make her
discontented; for that's the size of it.
She is so much stronger than I, however,
that it is she who has made me hate my
vacuous existence. O Felix," he groaned,
"there's only one way of looking at this
thing. If she had any man to stand up for
her, I should be horse-whipped to-morrow,
and serve me right. Even now, selfish
brute that I am, I believe it is my own
loss I am whining about, more than her
humiliation."

"She is very young, only a child," I suggested, by way of a crumb of cold comfort;
"she will get over it."

"I doubt it; she's so different from
everybody else, so situated that she will
have nothing to do but to think. She is
womanly, too; royal in unselfishness, and
I know she will be royal in suffering."
He drew a long breath, ending in a sigh.
"Good-night, Felix."

He was shivering from head to foot. "I

am not going to leave you to-night, Geoff.
I could n't sleep — and what are chums
for ?   Shut that window, and let 's light
a fire.   That beastly fog has penetrated
everything."

"What a good fellow you are, Felix!"
exclaimed Geoffrey, watching me kindle
the fire.   "How little I consider you!
What do I know of your troubles?   It is
enough for me that I wear you out with
mine, — you who work early and late, and
I who dawdle away an empty life."

"None of that now, Geoff Trevor," I
burst forth.   "As if I did n't know of all
your substantial kindnesses to my mother
and sisters.   You have been more to them
and to me than any man living ; and if
there were only gratitude to prompt, I
should be in your debt forever."

"Don't!" said Geoffrey.   "For God's
sake, don't!"   He sat up near, almost *in*,
the fire, for his teeth were chattering, and
shivers ran over him.   His elbows were
on his knees, and his head in his hands.
We talked no more ; but sat there, Geoff-
frey occasionally moaning, or changing his
position, until the day broke, — another

drizzling morning, but cold and raw, and devoid of beauty, this time. The fog-season had begun, — the bane of that coast. Geoffrey, looking like a ghost, went up with me in the train, to make some arrangements for Helen's coming. He intended to go down at night, see Alice for the last time, and abase himself "as low as he could crawl," before her, he said. But he had taken a violent cold ; and in the afternoon a message came for me to go to him at the Club. I found him in bed suffering horribly with rheumatism, to which he was subject.

He was so nervous that he made himself much worse. Would I go right down to Quartz, he begged, see Alice, and tell her that he was a trifle under the weather, and would n't be down for a day or two?

"Not unless I can tell her more," I replied. "To go down with a little temporizing message like that would be only to make matters worse. I am not asked to Murray's house, so I should have to go down on purpose to see Alice, and it would be very pointed, and make the deception more lingering and cruel. I would write her a note, though, so that she might not be in too great suspense," I told him.

"At my dictation, then. 'My dear Alexia,'" he began, — "' My dear Alexia : my — ' Well, I've got that half-a-dozen times. 'My dear Alexia : I have a touch of rheumatism, and cannot walk, so I shall not be able to go down to Quartz to-night to talk to you about — ' "

" No, I would n't say that, Geoff."

" Well, what would you say, then ? 'Go down to-night to correct your German exercise with you — ' "

" No, Geoff, that 's worse."

" 'Go down to-night as I had promised, no — hoped, no — intended to do. But I shall see you again in a day or two.'"

I laid down the pen. " That 's awful ! " It made a kind of rheumatic rhyme.

" O Heaven ! " groaned Geoffrey, with a twinge of conscience, or rheumatism, I don't know which. " Write it yourself, won't you ? "

So I worded a careful note, saying that he wished to see her, and would be down as soon as he was well enough. The expressman on the train promised to deliver it that evening. I pressed it into his hand, with solemn injunctions, and a sum of money, myself. Geoffrey would n't trust Murray either to give it to Alice, or to keep it to himself, he said.

The attack lasted four or five days; but on Saturday, so weak he could hardly stand, and so lame he could hardly walk, Geoffrey went down to Quartz. He must go, if it killed him, he said. It was his last chance: there were no Sunday trains; and on Monday Helen would arrive.

The situation was not altogether jovial, — Helen on her way home with her dead mother; Alice waiting for a mortal blow; Geoffrey, staggering with sickness and shame, starting to inflict the wound, and a worse one to himself at the same time.

VII.

LAURA TREVOR had carried out her plan of providing means to keep Alice in-doors, and a pile of unneeded garments had been hastily shaped for the purpose. Geoffrey, to be sure, had not appeared, but he might at any moment. Laura had not heard that he was disqualified for mischief just then, and to tell the truth, she laid his absence to fickleness or forgetfulness, and rather resented it.

Poor Alice had a hard three days of it, and then rebelled. "I can earn more money by rowing, dear Sister," she said beseechingly, "and sewing so much gives me a perfectly *awful* headache!" This to the apparently implacable Ignatia.

"But the work must be done, my child," urged Ignatia, who was not really severe at all; "and it is not only foolish, but wicked, to leave it half done."

"Then I'll pick it out," retorted Alice, with defiance in her eye, "and it won't be half done."

Sister Ignatia gave Alice a reproachful look, and Alice thereupon hugged her.

Early next morning the green dory was out, and the young victor in her red cap and handkerchief pulling for dear life, rejoicing in her liberty like a bird set free.

But her liberty was all she rejoiced in, poor child! and she was terribly unhappy. She worried vaguely about Geoffrey, whom she also missed every moment. He had been queer and dismal Sunday night, and had told her that he was going away. She had been so surprised and so shocked that she had cried; and then he had comforted her, and said he was not going yet. The next day she had had a note in another handwriting saying that he was ill.

Of course, she said to herself, he had been told, as she had been that Sunday, that it was wrong for them to be so much together; and for her sake — to save her trouble — he was going away. How noble, how generous, of him!

She waited, to let herself be hopelessly
miserable, until after the explanation he
had promised her. It was four days now,
and he had not come. She found herself
looking over her shoulder every moment,
and a man's footstep behind her made
her heart bound. But disappointments
were so frequent that by and by she began
to be discouraged. It seemed a year since
Sunday. The grass seemed to fade; it
was n't green any more, and there was less
of it; the water was no longer blue nor
sparkling; or if it was blue, and sparkled
so aggressively that she could n't help
noticing it, it made her feel worse than
ever.

The sunsets gave her no joy, and she
was sick of life. She was ashamed of herself for not having more heroism and more
faith, but she could n't help it. Sister Ignatia was her great comfort. Her head
was in the Sister's lap every night, and the
Sister pretending not to see the tears. One
night she had to speak.

"Sister," she said, throwing her arms
about the little woman's neck in one of
those wild, childish caresses which the Sis-

ter hardly dared own were precious to her,
and for the enjoyment of which she prayed
daily for forgiveness, " I was born to sad-
ness. I hope I shall learn to bear it
better."

" You were born to heavenly joys," answered the Sister, softly, stroking Alice's
hair. " You are happy in the promise of
them, are you not?"

" Yes," said the girl, hiding her head in
the folds of her protector's dress, " I hope
I am. But not like you, darling. I am
afraid I like earthly joys best." The
Sister shuddered. " You know for years
I fought against that wicked hatred of
my father, because he was a bad man,
and because he deserted me. That has
gone entirely, and now I have another
enemy."

" Who is that, Alexia ?"

" You mean *what* is it, dear. It is
something else in me. Oh, why, *why* is it
wrong," she burst forth, sitting up now
with hair all tumbled about, and eyes
bright and wild, " to love men ; to watch
for them, and long for them, when they
don't come, and to worry when they are

sick?" Her supposititious case was naïvely put.

"It will not be wrong for you, my child, to love a man, when the proper time comes, and to marry him."

"No, no!" said Alice. "I don't wish to marry. Yet I love," she murmured, hiding her face again.

"Hush!" exclaimed Sister Ignatia, laying her hand on Alice's lips, and looking greatly shocked. "You don't know what you say. I had hoped, Alexia, that with your serious thoughts, and your veneration for the religious life, you might one day feel it to be your vocation. But if it please God to send you a husband —"

It was Alice's turn now to hush the Sister. "Oh, don't," she cried; "I hate that horrid word husband, for I can never marry, never, never! Yet I love," she repeated, slowly this time, and as if she were no longer ashamed of it.

"Those are wicked words," exclaimed Sister Ignatia, fairly roused, and trying to push Alice away.

But Alice held her down. "Hear me," she begged, "only hear me!"

"Never," struggled the irate Ignatia, "while you speak that which your lips should never utter, nor my ears hear."

Alice smiled a sad, weary smile. "I shall not be asked to marry," she said, with proud pathos. "I am unworthy of the man I love. He could not love me. He is a nobleman, — rich, good, and handsome. What am I? I don't even know what I am [Sister Ignatia had never seen a trace of bitterness in the girl before], — the daughter of a criminal — perhaps of two; I am a miserable, low-born " — she hesitated for a word — " *thing,*" she added at last, with scornful emphasis ; " if it had not been for you, I should be digging worms at this minute, or mending tackle. Perhaps I should be in prison."

The woman was still pinioned by the girl's arms. "I have been blind," she cried, " and very, very wrong; I should have foreseen, prevented this. You may talk of noblemen, Alexia ; but there is nothing noble in a man who comes day after day, and lures a sweet, innocent girl on to love him, when he cannot love her."

"No!" cried the girl, springing to her feet, her eyes flashing flame. "I forbid you to say it! He has done nothing wrong. I have known from the first that he ruled my heart, and that I never could rule his. It has been *my* sin alone, all mine. And I have been absolved a hundred times, only to sin again. I love him," she burst forth again, with twitching lips and a broken voice. "I love him, in despair, in torment, but *I love him!*" She threw herself upon the hard floor, and sobbed and moaned. After all, Alexia was only a child, and this would do her good. It was the best symptom she had seen, the Sister said. She was very young to be in such trouble, and it was a mercy she could cry like that.

On Friday Alice got another little note, in Geoffrey's own handwriting this time. It was an off-hand effusion, penned with great labor! It remarked that the time had been long since he had seen her, that he hoped she had enjoyed the lovely days, and had slept through the lovely nights, —

or words to that effect. " I shall be down
on Saturday," it ended (Alice's heart
thumped her nearly out of the boat !) ; " so
be at Blynn's at four, with the green
dory."

She read the note over every few minutes during that day and the next, and
kissed it, and cried on it, and smiled at it,
and talked to it. Life would be over after
to-morrow, for of course there was to be a
parting ; but she could crowd whole years
of happiness into one hour, and live forever on the memory of it.

On Saturday at three o'clock (it was
just two minutes' walk to the wharf, and
Geoffrey was expected at four) Alice, so
excited that she could n't stay in the
house, took her tam-o'-shanter, and started
out.

"Where are you going?" inquired Sister Ignatia. Alice had not told her of the
note ; she was desperately afraid of being kept away from Geoffrey. Something
in Alice's manner had · aroused Ignatia's
suspicion.

" To Blynn's," she said, reddening furi-
ously, " to meet Mr. Geoffrey Trevor."

"I forbid it!" said the Sister, calmly, withdrawing to avoid argument. Alice did not quite dare disobey, and frantic with disappointment, she rushed to her room, feeling that the end of days had come for her.

VIII.

SO Geoffrey, in a flutter of emotions, — joy, grief, and gout, — went down to Quartz, — for the last time, he said to himself repeatedly; everything he did now was for the last time. But he would think only of beholding that incomparable loveliness once more, and not of losing sight of it. Let every minute take care of itself. He might not live to get away from her. He was a miserable object, this same Geoffrey, when he found no Alice at the wharf. Such a contingency had not occurred to him, and for a moment everything was black, and swam before his eyes. Old Iron was shuffling about, and he asked him where Alice was.

"Don't ask me," snapped the old man, querulously, and in an injured tone. "Them Sisters has kep' her nearly the hull o' this blessed week. I aint skurcely seed 'er. They's sing'lar doin's a-goin' on,

an' I aint got nothin' to do with 'em.
Sister Ignatia says to me, she says, ' Elixir
is a-goin' to be with us this week,' she
says, 'for sewin' an' offices;' offices is
prayers, sir" (seeing Geoffrey's puzzled
expression). " Alice she comes home, wal,
she comes home oncet or twicet a day,
but is off agin in one minute. I would n't
'a' let 'em had 'er, to eddicate 'er, ef I'd
'a' knowed they was a-goin' to keep 'er
like this. Don't ask me where she is. I
don't know nothin' about her."

This last was evidently a formula ; but
long before the old man had arrived at
that, Geoffrey was limping off in the direction of the Sisters' abode.

Alice saw him coming, and ran down to
the door to meet him. They stood looking
at each other, both hearts beating like
hammers.

Alice was more radiantly exquisite than
ever, he thought ; once or twice, during the
week, he had lost sight of her face completely ; it is often so with those we love.
Oh, how beautiful she was, and how true,
and what a joy it was to look upon her
· dear face again !

"Put on your hat, Alexia, and come out for a row," he said. Somehow it seemed unnatural for them to be out of a boat.

"I can't," said Alice.

"Can't? Why not? Are you a prisoner?"

A tall thin Sister, Dorothea, — the one Geoffrey had never seen, — came to the door, hearing a man's voice. She bowed gravely to Geoffrey, and standing as if to receive any message he might have to impart, told Alice to go in.

"Oh, but I came to see her," said Geoffrey, making a pathetic attempt at being jovial, "and I have asked her to go out with me. I have something of importance to say to her."

"Can the business not be transacted here?" asked Sister Dorothea. She was severe to men on general principles only, and did not know the horror with which this particular one should be regarded.

"Not very well," returned Geoffrey, smiling. He was not pleased, all the same; in fact, he was very much annoyed. 'Suppose she should insist upon knowing what the business was! A nice thing it would be to tell, that he had come down to stab Alice to the heart; and a fine chance of seeing her alone it would afford him!

He felt his strength, too, which was purely nervous, leaving him rapidly. What if he should become suddenly helpless, as he had done last Monday! He leaned heavily upon his stick, as he tried to think up a stratagem by which he might gain Alice's ear privately.

"I will row you over," broke in Alice, boldly. "You look very ill." And she started off at once, Geoffrey following, and blessing her for her stroke. She did n't wait to get her cap, for fear of more obstacles.

So they were together again. Instead of going to the pier, where interruptions and encounters would be sure to await them, they strolled in the direction of the Head. Geoffrey hardly dared look at the sweet, precious thing beside him. He knew how she must be looking. Every glance he had ever given her had found her lovelier; had disclosed new delights. Her beauty pervaded the air; he felt it all about him. So far from enjoying these precious moments, however, every one gave a keener pain; it was one nearer the last,—O God! the end.

When they were beyond the houses, he spoke. "Alexia," he said gently,—the name even was peculiar to her; no one else bore it,—"Alexia." She turned her face to him, ablaze with excitement and gladness. Oh, was ever anything harder than this? "I am here," she said encouragingly. She thought she knew what troubled him; and she would make it as easy as she could. He had not been to blame.

"Alexia," he began again,—to plan a "clean breast" is one thing; to make it so different!—"I have done a very wicked thing; several wicked things. May I make my confession to you?"

Alice turned pale. "No," she said, casting her eyes down, and speaking in a low tone; "make it to God."

"There is more chance of forgiveness there, perhaps," he answered bitterly. "But I have an explanation to make to you, Alexia, and I must make it now. Shall we sit down?"

How lame he was! how pale! how thin!
He must have suffered terribly, Alice
thought. They sat down on a large rock,
overlooking the bay and the coast and the
harbor. It was a lovely afternoon, although
there was a thick gray bank of fog creep-
ing in from outside; horribly lovely, it
seemed to Geoffrey. Every breath of the
fresh salt air, instead of giving him life, as it
used to do, gave him death. Nothing ever
was so beautiful as this that he was giving
up, — this jewel in its setting. Yet how
could he give up what he never had, and
never could have had? But the possibility
of possession had occurred to him, and that ·
is nine points of the law to some men.

Alice wore now a bewildered, anxious air.
It was different from what she thought it
was going to be. An hour of present, with
a month of past and a possible half-century
of future attached to it, never can give pure
joy. Only babies, fools, and philosophers
can separate one hour from the tangle of
life, and live in it. Alice realized that fact
unconsciously and vaguely then.

She could not believe that Geoffrey had
committed any crime. If he meant de-

ceiving her, she could quickly set his mind
at rest on that point. He had not deceived her; because from the first, as she
had told Sister Ignatia, she had known *perfectly* that gentlemen like him did not love
girls like her; they could n't; they never
thought of such a thing; they just liked
them, and were very kind to them. Hers
was the crime, if you like, for letting herself go on loving him, when she knew all
the time how worse than vain it was. She
only waited now for an opportunity to say
this to him, and to lift the load, if it was
that which troubled him. Why did he not
speak and let her do it?

Great drops were standing on Geoffrey's
forehead. It was with difficulty he spoke
at all. He had rehearsed nothing coming
down, except that he would tell her of his
love for her, as a guaranty of good faith,
that she might know how desperately in
earnest he had been, how far from trifling
with her. The confession would condemn
his head, but not his heart, which was
hers; and this was the second part of his
programme, — that he would refuse to see,
would ignore utterly, the fact that she

loved him. If she had a secret of her own she should keep it, and his too. He would not spare himself, but he would shield her.

He plunged in at last. "Alexia," he said again, "I had never loved a woman in my life when I asked one to marry me a few months ago."

It was badly worded, and she misunderstood him. "You mean *until* you asked her to marry you?" she said softly. It was an awful blow, but she bore it well.

"No, I mean *when* — *at the time* — I asked her, and after — and until — *now*," he gasped, afraid of frightening her away if he said too much.

But she was perplexed again. "I don't think I understand you," she said. "'The wicked thing' you mean was asking her to — marry you, when you did n't love her?"

"That was one, yes. I had been a miserably selfish, morbid man, and I thought I could make her happy, and I made up my mind to devote my life to her — at least, I *think* I thought so; I meant to think so. I don't know exactly what I did think, but I did it."

"Does she know it? I mean, does she know that you did n't love her, when you — then ?"

"Never mind her," answered Geoffrey, gently. "She has not suffered yet; I doubt if she ever does. She will not know. The next wicked thing I did was to fall madly in love with somebody else " (he saw her start, turn deadly pale, and shiver), "as I have done, Alexia, wretched, wretched man that I am!"

"Oh, can't you help it? Can't you fight against it?" exclaimed Alice, in real anguish. She had n't against hers, to be sure; but then he was strong. And now that she knew he loved, she *would* overcome hers! Her own trouble was forgotten in his; the sight of his emotion was terrible to her; tears streamed down her cheeks.

"You did n't mean to do it," she pleaded. " I know you would not do a wrong thing. And if you do not tell the girl — the lady — that you — love her, there is no crime; I mean, if you repent. It is not as bad as you think; everybody has to suffer; you must live more for heaven; it will all be over by and by!"

How glad she was, even in the midst of her distress, that she was not in the condition of life where ladies and gentlemen married without love! She had longed to be a lady, lately, but she would n't now be one for the world! It was so revolting, so horrible, and she ought to tell *him* so, to take lies upon their lips at the altar; to profane a holy sacrament! After all (her heart gave a bound), it was a simple matter to set things straight; it was only a question of right and wrong. He had no right to marry, not loving; he must go to the first one and tell her so; and he must marry the other. It was her duty to put this plainly before him, and she would.

But oh, in spite of her kind heart and her disregard of self, what were these she felt, — these sharp twinges shooting across her at the thought of the girl he — O God! — he loved.

While Alice's plan was shaping itself, Geoffrey had been in a perfect daze. That such unconsciousness, such utter ignoring of self, could exist, had never by any chance occurred to him. He had known Alice to be lacking in vanity, but this — why, this was the meekness of — why, he dared not think what it was! She was not of the earth. His torture grew every instant ; it seemed coarse now to tell her of his love, and yet he loved her to agony. An impulse seized him.

"Alexia! darling!" He clutched her hand. She should not go until he had finished. "Don't you know? Can't you see? It is *you*, sweet, I love. I did not know it till it burst upon me. I am dying for love of you. But I belong to — others. So I have come to say good-by to you, and to beg you to forgive me for daring to insult you so."

In spite of her struggles to release herself, and his weakness, he still held her hand. He saw the burst of joy which brought the blood bounding in a torrent to her cheeks ; he could hardly control himself. In one moment more he would have defied Helen and the world, and would have implored Alice to fly with him in the green dory !

But she wrenched her hand away. "Let me go," she said; and no effort of hers could disguise the rapture in her tone. "I love you, too," she murmured, "and I can suffer with joy and gladness now to the end of my life." She had started at her first words, and now she was gone like the wind.

There, on the rock, where Alice had left him, sat Geoffrey for another hour. He had not tried to follow her; for he knew he must not see her again — ever.

He was in a whirl of confused emotions; he did n't know how or what he felt most. To find her so noble and so strong added to the pain of non-possession; and yet he felt he had presumed in daring to love this lowly fisher-maiden, so far, far above him was she. Her kindness to him, poor little broken-hearted comforter! before she knew he loved her, had been nothing short of heavenly charity; angels could have done no more.

But oh! the blessed thought that cheered him, as it had glorified her, — the knowledge of her love, — all his! The burden somehow had been lessened, the weight of guilt grown lighter. They bore a common sorrow. For a moment he was almost happy at the thought that their sufferings were exactly alike. Yet the differences forced themselves into prominence, every now and then, and his sense of guilt returned.

It took Geoffrey, in his worn-out condition, a long time to go to the station, and then he found that the last train had gone. He was not up to the exertion of driving to the nearest town, to take one there; so he hired a man to drive him over the dusty dyke to Murray's house. It was much farther than the old way, but he would not go near the harbor, lest Alice should be there. She must be placed in no embarrassing position now by him.

Laura was lying in a long chair, in the veranda. She was surprised to see Geoffrey, but not overjoyed. She had just heard of his illness. "You poor cripple!" she exclaimed; "tell them to bring another long chair over here, and we'll groan together, and exchange notes on symptoms. It has been a bad week, so foggy and damp; and now I see there is another big bank rolling in."

Geoffrey declined the offer of the long chair, but sank rather hard into the most comfortable one near him. "Where's Murray?" he asked, by way of something to say. He dreaded seeing him, he was so tactless.

"I don't know, I'm sure; he has n't gone sailing, because he was afraid of the fog, but he will be half a day late to dinner, as usual; so let's have ours. I am lucky to secure a vis-à-vis."

So they dined, and carefully avoided every subject but the most remote; and it was a dull dinner.

Murray came in, full of excuses, when they had nearly finished. The fog was getting so thick, he said, they could hardly get across the harbor. "Blame this fog!" said Murray; "it puts an end to everything. I hoped we had had enough of it; but we're in for another bout of a week, I suppose."

IX.

SUNDAY came, raw and rainy, and with a dense fog shrouding everything. Geoffrey was glad of the excuse his rheumatism gave him to stay in-doors, for although it would be hard to find anybody in such a fog, he wished not to run the risk of worrying Alice with an encounter. It was a dull, dreary day, — not a sign of a town, or a boat, or even a bay, had been seen. Toward evening, by the clock, — for there was only a degree more darkness than there had been, — old Iron came clattering up the veranda steps, and, with every appearance of ague, fairly fell into the room where they were all sitting.

"My God!" he roared, without preface, — the first time in his life he had been direct, — "you aint seen the child, hev you, anybody? She's out in the fog, an' she's ben out sence last night, an' I'm

9

afeared she's starved or froze, ef she aint drownded!"

They had all sprung to their feet at the first words ; and before Iron had finished, Murray and Geoff, followed by the trembling old fisherman and some small boys, were stalking down to the float. As universal a resort, a wharf, in a place like this, at such a time, as a police-station in the city.

A servant came running after Geoffrey with a great-coat. "Mrs. Trevor sent this to you, sir, and begs you to be careful; she says you must not stay out in the damp."

Geoffrey threw the coat aside in a fury. The very idea of his thinking of his own health at such a time! He only hoped he could die, saving her! He was almost insane.

Old Iron, after seventeen preambles and a hundred digressions, explained as he tumbled, breathless, down the road after the others, that the reason he had n't missed Alice before was because he thought she was with the Sisters ; and the reason the Sisters had n't missed her was because they thought she was with him.

Everybody was out in boats now, large and small, with horns and without them ; but the thickness of the fog prevented a real search, and one or two of the men got lost for hours, going too far to look. All they could do was to row about in a desultory way, blowing the horns, and shouting. There was not a puff of wind. Old Iron said he never had seen such a fog, and he was about the oldest inhabitant.

Murray was the coolest hand in the whole party ; he insisted that Alice was level-headed, and that when she found herself fog-bound she had gone ashore at the nearest place, or had boarded some vessel. The thought of her alone, however, at the mercy of stray sailors, was death and distraction to Geoffrey.

Although the fog might account for Alice's absence, — and he hugged that hope, — Geoffrey from the first had feared suicide. She could not bear her trouble, he said to himself. Elopement had been Sister Ignatia's explanation of the disappearance, but here was Geoffrey ; and Blynn had seen Alice take the green dory, and row very hard toward the mouth of the harbor. He thought of "warnin' of her then," Blynn said, but "it was one of those things you think of doin' and don't!"

Seeing Geoffrey's distress, Sister Ignatia forbore to give him her opinion of his conduct. He frankly told her that Alice had run away from him, and what he dreaded, knowing her agitation. Alexia would never commit suicide, the Sister proudly affirmed; she had been too well taught for that. She looked upon it as the most horrible and unpardonable of all crimes, to take her soul, unasked, into the presence of its Possessor. Alexia was a God-fearing child, and she would trust her as she would trust herself.

The fog did not lift, and the town was in an uproar all night. In the morning I got a telegram from Geoffrey, asking me to go and meet Helen at the steamer. "Alice is missing," it said.

The position was not one I should have sought, and how on earth to account for Geoff's absence from his post puzzled me, I can tell you.

Before the message reached me, probably, there was a lifting of the fog, and a

small sloop yacht was discovered, making
for the harbor, and towing a green dory!
A man and two women were discerned
standing in the stern, and one of them,
leaping to the bow, and waving her handkerchief, was then observed to be Alice.

It turned out to be as Murray had said.
Alice had taken her boat for a long,
long spin, forgetting all about the fog,
which had surrounded her near Melancholy
Island. Seeing, from a long intimacy with
fogs, the vanity of trying to get back, she
had drawn the dory up on the beach of
the island, and spent the night in it. In
the morning she had rowed cautiously,
a few feet at a time, and shouting every
instant. This gentleman and his wife had
heard her at last; and after many false
turns, for the fog was deceptive, as well
as dense, she had found their yacht, and
got on board. And then they had been
at anchor, like every other sailing craft
about, ever since, for fear of rocks and
collisions.

Geoffrey did not wait to speak to Alice.
Nobody would notice, in the confusion,
whether he did or not, and he would not

disturb her any more. He saw her as she landed. Her hair was wet with vapor, and clinging about her forehead in rings; her eyes were scared and solemn; and her lips were quivering, at the thought of the trouble she had caused. It took all Geoffrey's self-control, and more too, to keep him from rushing forward, taking her in his arms, and holding her there forever. Murray said he looked sixty years old.

It was too late now to meet Helen, but he could drag himself to her house, and patch up matters somehow. The night in the drenching mist, and his worry and self-reproach had not improved Geoffrey's physical condition, and he was really very ill. But he had his work yet to do, and he nerved himself to do it.

At the station in the city Geoffrey took a cab and hurried off. "She is not dead," he repeated to himself, — "not dead. But oh, that night on Melancholy Island! All my fault, my own darling, every bit; from now on, every one of your sufferings I, who adore you, shall have caused. Oh, it was all too horrible and bad and beastly!" and he cursed himself over and over again.

When the cab stopped at Helen's door, Geoffrey had almost forgotten what he had come for. He climbed the steps stiffly and slowly, and rang the bell. Murray had poured brandy down his throat and forced him to swallow his coffee, and he had made his toilet mechanically; but he bore traces still of having been out all night, and he felt that deadly ache in his bones which none but the truly rheumatic know.

The servant who opened the door, and who bore marks of recent weeping, looked shocked at seeing him. Miss Helen had arrived, but could see nobody; which rather surprised Geoffrey, as the man knew him perfectly, and his position in the house. He sent up his card, however, and waited.

Presently the servant returned, bearing a note, with a black border an inch deep. Geoffrey took it with strange sensations of joy and guilt, — guilt at the joy, I think. Then she would not see him!

"I cannot forgive your extraordinary conduct," the note ran, "in not coming to meet me; and I decline to see you."

This was vague, and whether it amounted

to a dismissal or not, Geoffrey could n't tell. He could take it for one, however, and he would. Then it was true; he was free, free to go to — "Oh no, no, *no*," he cried out; he had no right to take Helen at her word; of course his conduct had seemed barbarous to her without an explanation, and of course he must do his best to reinstate himself with her.

He wrote on the blank half-sheet of her letter, and the mourning border seemed singularly appropriate :—

My dear Helen, — I can explain to you why I seemed so unnatural this morning. Nothing would have kept me but a matter of life and death. Let me see you and tell you about it, I beg,

Yours ever,   Geoffrey.

This sent off, he was plunged into despair again, because he knew she must listen to his appeal !

In a moment the man returned, and said Miss Helen would be in the drawing-room directly. So Geoffrey went up, and awaited her in a company of sheeted ghosts, for the furniture was in its summer garments,—most fitting associates for him just then,—and Helen, in billows of black, swept in. She was overcome, very much, at seeing him; and Geoffrey was touched by the weariness in her face. It had been an awful experience for her, poor girl! he thought, and he was glad he had conquered himself.

"You look fearfully ill, Geoffrey," she said in a constrained manner, yet kindly. "What *is* the matter with you?"

"Oh, nothing," Geoffrey replied, "only a touch of the gout."

I think for a moment Helen may have thought he had made her troubles his. But that was rather beyond her powers of comprehension.

"What I want to say to you is this, Helen," Geoffrey said. "At the very moment I should have been starting to meet you this morning, we were scouring the bay to find the grandchild of Murray Trevor's old fisherman, who had been missing since Saturday." How lame it sounded as he said it! He had not realized how flimsy his excuse really was. I had when I made it to Helen on the steamer, and saw her face! Of course he could hardly explain to her his violent interest in the girl.

"The *grandchild of Murray Trevor's old fisherman!* And you come here, in sober earnest, to tell me that you desert me in my hour of need and affliction, because a dirty little baby down at Quartz Head falls into the water! And pray, who has constituted *you* the guardian of that town?" she sneered. "You never saw it till a month ago. And were there not relations of the child to search for it, without you, who were bound by every tie of decency to come to me? The grandchild of Murray Trevor's fisherman! Oh, it's monstrous, Geoffrey! It's not to be borne." And she turned to leave him.

Again Geoffrey's heart leaped. Had he not done all he could, and failed? No, he must push it to the end. Only he would not pretend to care much; it was too sickening to go on deceiving; he could n't do it. But he made another effort.

"Very well, Helen," he said gravely, "if you choose to misunderstand. I could not have come to you, nor to my own sister, when a young girl was perhaps drowning or drowned. I had been last with her on the evening she disappeared, and it would have been indecent for me to come away until the fate of the girl was known. It was not a baby, nor a child ; it was a girl of seventeen, and a remarkably fine girl at that."

How he hated himself for speaking so of her ! The adjective was well chosen, he might have used it of a chambermaid ; and Helen was mollified before he had finished his plea. She had been hard upon him ; one ought never to condemn so hastily, and she told him so. "Of course, Geoffrey," she said, putting out her hand, " I was terribly wounded at your not being at the wharf to receive me; it seemed so heartless; and your friend, Mr. Farley, made such an insufficient apology for you. [I did n't know what to say, confound it !] But I will forgive you, dear, and we 'll say no more about it. The first thing to do is to get you well. I must stay with you always now."

Oh, how loathsome his position was ! How was he ever going to live on like this ?

He must speak the truth out now. He had seen how fatal delays were, in the case of Alice; and drifting along irresponsibly with tide and current was all very well, when you had not to get back, against both. It was a shocking time to cause Helen pain, with her mother lying dead in the house; but *must* he not speak? Was that not the only course?

It was only for her he cared; *he* was indifferent to everything; but he must end her deception, if she were deceived. She had never loved him; so it could n't matter much really to her.

"Helen," he said, in a low voice, approaching her and speaking in a gentle, pained manner, "I have never loved you as a man should do who is to become your husband. I think you have always known this, or you did know it once; but you said you were content with what I could give you, and that you did not believe in the grand passion yourself. I am right?"

Helen had turned her back partly around, and was nervously fingering a vase on the chimney-piece. She made no answer.

"I honestly think — for I must make

some slight plea for myself — that if you had not gone away, things would have remained exactly as they were. That *should* have made no difference, I suppose, to a man of honor, but it did — to me. You did go ; and I — since you have been gone — I — have fallen in love!"

Helen wheeled round and faced him, her eyes blazing, her chest heaving, with scorn and wrath. "A 'man of honor' — *you!*" Her contempt was withering. "So, sir," measuring him from head to foot, " this is the man to whom I have given myself! This the — "

Geoffrey stopped her. " Don't, Helen ; I don't blame you for being disgusted ; but listen one moment. I have done you no *outward* wrong. [He knew her vulnerable point.] I still hold myself yours ; do as you please with me ; take me, or leave me." She should have the initiative, he thought.

" A fine possession, truly, to take or leave," sneered Helen, again glaring at Geoffrey. Her face was ghastly pale, with a burning red spot on each cheek, and her eyes were glittering. She bit her lip to keep the tears of anger back. "A noble type; a perfect gentleman! So, sir, it is mine, is it, — this gem, this pearl of great price?" She hesitated, crouching for a spring. "Very well, then, it shall continue mine, poor paltry thing that it is! [Geoffrey started, as if he were shot; he could not believe his ears.] Your name and your protection are mere commodities to me now, but they will be useful to me; at any rate, it serves my purpose to keep them. Your love you may bestow where you choose; I scorn it. But I will not be humiliated before the world." And she swept to the door.

"Helen," cried out Geoffrey, — "Helen, you shall not go like this, Helen! You are not fit to discuss the point now. I should not have brought it up. Helen!"

But she was gone, and all Geoffrey could do was to go too. What a fiend she was! And he had crawled at her feet, and she had set her foot upon his neck and pressed him farther into the earth. He was still bound to her, but with every moral tie broken. Nothing but handcuffs held them together now.

X.

GEOFFREY broke down altogether. I never saw him so ill. He staggered into my rooms that afternoon. He could not go to the Club, he said, he must be near me ; and he never left my bed for a fortnight. He was entirely prostrated, poor Geoff! and for days he never opened his eyes. He suffered intensely, but he bore it like a hero.

I sent Miss Courtice word that he would not be able to go to the funeral ; and Murray took his place. The day after old Mrs. Courtice was buried, Helen herself appeared, swathed in crape, to minister to Geoffrey. I saw her, and told her that the doctor had given orders he was to see no one, and indeed he was too sick. She begged me to send her word when she could come to help nurse him. I did n't know then what had happened, but I thought I had never seen such a cold, hard face in so young a woman. She looked very handsome; and the nurse, who saw her too, told Geoffrey he ought to be very proud to have such a lovely lady coming to inquire for him. Geoffrey managed to call up a heartrending smile, like the dying ray of a winter sunset ; and I told the nurse not to let him know of any more visitors. One night, when he was half delirious, he beckoned me to him, and told me, in a solemn whisper, that he was afraid of Helen!

It was when we were alone — or the faithful attendant was snoring — that Geoffrey told me all that had happened at Quartz, with Alice, and in town. The hot tears came into his eyes as he spoke of Alice, but he loved to talk about her, and I knew he was always thinking of her. He said he wanted to live and suffer, so as to be worthy of her. If it had not been for her, whom he should never see again, he would have longed to die. His life had been such a wretched waste, he said ; but he was going to try to repair it, — to do what she would have him do.

Murray Trevor came in every day, and was very anxious about Geoffrey. "I believe there *was* something between him and Alice, Farley," said the old stupid to me one day, as I was letting him out. "You were right. She's going to take a veil, or be a nun, or something. Old Iron told me so. She has promised him that she'll wait till the autumn, though. He's in a deuce of a way about it."

As Geoffrey grew stronger, and was beginning to sit up, there seemed to be no way of keeping Helen out any longer, so we let her come. Geoffrey treated her with deference, but nothing more. She was very uncomfortable, but her manner was kind and devoted before me. She was behaving so badly that Geoffrey had not one ray of respect for her, and of course it was monstrous to let the thing go on. One night I put out a feeler.

"Geoff," I said, "haven't you almost fulfilled your duty to that lump of black ice, that frowning crag, who comes here every day, to prevent you from getting well?"

He shook his head wearily. "No," he said sadly. "The more unhappy I am, the greater is my expiation, I feel."

"Oh, stuff and grandmother!" I exclaimed, out of all patience. "What good does your leading a dog's life do either of those two women? It grieves one to death, and fosters a wrong spirit in the other. As you are going on now, you are simply pandering to Helen Courtice's thirst for vengeance. She is wretched, — anybody can see that; you are a thousand times more so; and as for that poor, patient soul down at Quartz Head, who is going to retire from the world, she suffers more than both of you put together."

"Retire from the world! What do you mean?" cried the invalid, catching at that in an instant.

"Why, she's going to be a Sister, or something."

"How do you know?" He was growing excited; but the doctor had told me to try to rouse him.

"Murray Trevor told me so."

"When?"

"Oh, the other day. I thought it wiser not to tell you."

"Now, I say, Felix, don't keep things from me. *Pray* don't! I am perfectly well. I'm going out to-morrow. Tell me all about it, Felix."

I told him just what Murray had said.

" Does she know I have been sick?"

" Well, rather. She wrote me, and I have written her about you every day."

" You trump! you brick!" shouted Geoffrey, jumping up from his chair. " Let me see her letter, quick, there's a good fellow!"

I went and got it. He snatched it out of my hand, and actually trembled as he tore it open.

It was a little note; but he could n't have made more fuss over a quarto volume. It only said: —

DEAR MR. FARLEY, — Mr. Murray Trevor has told my grandfather that Mr. Geoffrey is very ill. Will you let me know how ill? And if there is *anything* I can do, may I, please, do it?

Respectfully yours,

ALICE.

Geoffrey uttered a Romeo-like little moan as he closed the note, only to open it and devour it again a moment later.

" And so it sends her a bulletin every day, does it?" said Geoffrey, actually smiling. " O Felix ! Felix ! What can I ever do for you ? "

" Get well, and finish up that Courtice business," I retorted, rather coarsely I am afraid. It made me furious.

Geoffrey gained ; and one day he wrote Helen that he did n't feel he could claim her time or her attention any longer in his sick-room. " Let me know how I can serve you," he added, not knowing exactly what he meant, but giving her a loop-hole for a graceful exit.

Her answer was an insolent one : —

"I shall let you know, be sure, sir, how you can serve me. It is for no other purpose I keep up this farce, which does not amuse me in the least. But what you owe me you shall pay."

One morning, when he was about again, he went to see Helen. She was still in town, leading a secluded life ; in fact, seeing nobody. He started with the full determination not to leave her until he had made her see the situation aright, through his eyes. Above all, there should be no quarrel, if he could by any effort prevent it.

Geoffrey had changed very much ; there was not a trace of the old cynicism about him ; he was trying to be good now for good's sake. It was Helen's happiness for which he was honestly striving ; not his own, nor Alice's, — which was, after all, his own. He could give up all hope of possessing Alice ; but he would never give up the hope of being worthy of her.

Helen had had a thoroughly bad training, thought Geoffrey. The greatest allowance must be made for her; the most infinite patience used with her. He *had* treated her ill, very ill, there was not a question of it, and of course she would be revengeful. So would he have been before he had had that shining example before him !

The trouble with Helen was that she was perfectly unreasonable. She seemed to think she could upbraid Geoffrey in the most cutting terms, — " call him everything," as the phrase is, — and yet command his willing service. She cared nothing for him, she openly avowed ; in fact, she hated him. The world's opinion, then, was far more to her than her own happiness.

"If, even after we were engaged, I had won your love, Helen," said Geoffrey to her, kindly, when the interview had already lasted more than an hour, "I would not think of changing the condition of affairs, provided you wished it to remain.   I would not consider myself, in any case. But why do I say, 'if I had won your love'?   If you had loved me, there would have been no such thing as temptation for me ; I should have been clothed in a coat of mail.   And then, too, if you had loved me, you would never have left me."   He could not resist putting in that plea for himself again.

"Oh, '*left*' you!" mocked Helen. "How tired I am of that eternal lament ! *Left* you!   What is it to go abroad, for Heaven's sake ?   No more than running down to Campobello, and you wanted me to do that !   As if a man could n't be 'left' for a week or two, for fear of his getting into mischief!   Besides, you could have gone with me — I'm sure I urged you enough — or followed me.   It is an absurdly babyish excuse for a grown man to make, that he was 'left all alone'!" And Helen made a grimace, like a child, or imitating one.

"Very well, then; we'll drop that; there shall be no more excuses. I have sinned against you deeply. I am going to make reparation. Reparation is *repairing* — the wrong I have done you; not persisting in it and rushing into ten times as much more, as you would have me do. God knows, for every pain I cause you I suffer a hundred; and that is no more than a just proportion." Oh, would this interview never end! It was such a brutal position to be in! If he was not reaping the whirl-wind with a vengeance! But it must be followed to the finish.

She admitted that her aims were vicious. She declared now that she wished to thwart Geoffrey; he was striving to be free from her, in order that he might marry this unprincipled creature, who had stolen him from her!

Geoffrey had made up his mind that Alice should not be brought into the con-troversy. He was roused now, however.

"If there were no other woman in the
world, Helen," he said, "it would be the
same now. It happens to be love which
brought me to my senses ; which opened
my eyes to the wickedness of our course.
It might have been anything else; it
would have come to the same thing, I
hope. Since the day you landed I have
not seen — the person you designate so
untruly, — for she is pure principle and
goodness ; I may never see her again. I
am simply viewing the thing in the light
of truth. I should be sinning most mon-
strously, if with this light full upon me I
allowed you to go on living a wicked
lie."

"I wonder this moral mirror, this em-
bodiment of all that is finest in woman
[this was the chance Helen had been
longing for] did not begin her great
work earlier, — by preventing you from
plunging into such mad devotion to her,
for instance," said Helen, with a hateful
smile. "She was slow in sowing the precious seed ; the crop came up rather late
in the season."

"Enough of her," said Geoffrey ; "she

has no place in this discussion. The matter rests on another basis altogether. I beg you, Helen, to break off this engagement (there is nothing left of it but a tattered cobweb) in your own way ; tell your friends as much or as little as you choose ; blame me freely; I will not open my mouth to justify myself. If every man in this town shuns me, it will be no more than my desert. I mean it when I say that I will bear my punishment."

" Yes, as long as one woman does not shun you," jeered Helen, "you can bear the loss of everything else." She drew herself up to her full height ; she was very tall. " I will not plead with you, sir, to marry me." Her face crimsoned with shame at the actual wording of the idea which she had implied repeatedly without a blush. "Go! I shall not soil my lips with the story of your ruffianly conduct. I only pray that the vulgar person you ' honor' with your manly preference may bring you to the dust; may cover you with shame, as you have brought — as you have covered — me ! "

Helen's fortitude, or bravado, forsook

her before she had finished. Tears — it mattered not if they were of rage ; they were womanly, and touched Geoffrey as her words had never done — choked her voice, and she was on the point of breaking down. As Geoffrey did not go, she moved toward the door. He placed himself directly before her. "No, Helen," he said ; "not with a curse on your lips. Bless me, rather, for saving you from a fearful fate. And, Helen," — tears choked *him* now, — "forgive me, *do* forgive me ! You must believe — you must *know* — that I am sincere ? O Helen, let me be your friend ! I can make you a good friend ; I should have made you a horrible husband ! "

Helen had covered her face with her hands ; her form was convulsed with sobs ; she was crying now like any broken-hearted woman. At last she put out her hand gropingly, and touched his arm.

"Forgive *me*," she sobbed ; "you are noble. I have always known it." And she burst by him through the doorway, and out.

The next week she sailed for England. A little note was thrust into her hand as she left. It was this : —

" May every joy be yours. And may the sins of him who wronged you first, but righted you afterward, be forgiven by your true self, — that self which was revealed in a flood of glory at the last. God bless you, Helen ! "

XI.

GEOFFREY maintained strict decorum for weeks. He sent Alice no line; and he tried hard not to think of her until the period of his "complimentary mourning," so to speak, had passed. He made it a long one; long enough to make me very nervous, for I was afraid Alice would take the veil before he could get there to prevent it.

One day, late in the summer, he went to Quartz. He would not have gone then (for Helen's sake), so bent was he upon being good (for Alice's), but that he had received news from England. Helen Courtice and Max Lorimer were engaged !

Then Geoffrey beamed. He laughed aloud; he sang ; he danced! He was the happiest man I ever saw. Now, now, after darkness and suspense and anguish, had come the dawn. The night of gloom had passed. He could open the shutters boldly now, and let in the cool, sweet, fragrant morning air!

I went down with him, for I thought somebody ought to break the news to the Trevors. And then my help might be required; for Geoffrey, who had been the soul of patience so long, had thrown off that disguise, and had declared to me, in an excited tone, that if Alice would do him that unspeakable honor, he should be married the very instant he got to Quartz, and saw her.

When we reached the little station again, and were winding through the crooked streets, the scene of Geoffrey's old joys and miseries, he showed great emotion. He could not realize his freedom, to begin with, and he looked as if he were bursting with it. He stalked on ahead, with long strides, to the Sisters' house. What if she were not there! What if something had happened to her! What if she would not marry him! His hand trembled, and his face was flushed, as he went up to the little black door, and pulled the bell-handle. I hoped the Sisters

would not think he had been drinking!
He had already vices enough in their eyes,
without that addition.

Sister Dorothea, grave and uncompro-
mising, opened the door. She was intimate
with the whole history of his misdemeanors
now, and no mistake should be made again
through her lack of vigilance! She looked
at Geoffrey very severely.

"Can I—Is Alexia here?" he gasped,
husky and out of breath.

"You may not see Sister—Alexia;"
she meant the last word for a correction,
but Geoffrey was appalled.

"Sister—wha-a-t did you say? I beg
your pardon," asked Geoffrey, in a faint
voice. "She has not become a Sister? I
was told not. But I *must* see her!"

"She is not a Sister yet," said Dorothea,
who looked more lightly upon the sin of
prevarication than usual, at that moment,
if I mistake not. "She has taken no
vows; but she has given me her promise
never to see you again, unless," she added,
without a smile, — "unless you are at the
point of death, which seems not to be the
case now."

It would be soon, I thought, if she kept him much longer in this suspense. It was agonizing to him.

"I must see her," he repeated peremptorily. "Please tell her that I am here."

Sister Dorothea stood her ground, without budging. She looked as if she were going to call a constable.

"I have come," said Geoffrey, taking off his hat, and speaking with great dignity and deliberation, "to ask Alexia to do me the great honor of becoming my wife. I do not deserve the distinction, I am well aware; but I must hear my fate from Alexia's own lips. Will you allow me to come in?"

The Sister, feeling herself vanquished, stepped aside. "I will go and find Alexia," she said, and went toward the stairway. It was a tiny little house.

"Oh, don't go up; call her," pleaded poor Geoffrey, piteously; and Dorothea, smiling, obeyed. As Alice's foot touched the top-stair, mine was on the gravel-walk outside; and I caught a glimpse of Sister Dorothea fleeing down the little passage which led to the back of the house.

I went directly over to the Trevors' house, to prepare Laura. I found out later what Geoffrey's mode of procedure was. After he and Alice had — well, seen each other for some time, Geoffrey asked Alice to come out with him at once, to find the clergyman, and be married. They had had a horrible separation, he said, and he wanted to end it, and look after her all himself, from that moment. But Alice declared such haste would be impossible ; she called the Sisters in at last, to sustain her in this view.

They were horrified. Marriage was a sacrament, Sister Ignatia said, and Alice must not rush into it without preparation. And then it was not canonical to be married after twelve o'clock.

" Very well," sighed Geoffrey, — he could not let go Alice's hand a moment, and his eyes were feasting on her face, — " the first thing in the morning, then, right after breakfast. I shall be ready by daylight."

" But Alexia has no white dress," Sister Ignatia demurred, " and we must make her one."

"I could telegraph to town, and have some sent down, if I wanted her to wear one," said the lordly bridegroom, "but I don't. I wish her to wear the flannel gown I have always seen her in," he said, eying with great disfavor the black one she wore, and gently removing her white cap.

"Oh, dreadful!" exclaimed Sister Ignatia. "She *shall not* be married in that flannel. And then the veil; she must have a veil!"

"No," said Geoffrey, decidedly, determined to score one point, — "no veil. I don't want her rigged up at all. I like her in her hair best;" and the unconventional swain actually drew the young lady to him, and kissed her, ignoring the bystanders.

"But, Mr. Trevor," urged the gentle little Sister, "it is not permitted a woman to enter the church without a covering for her head."

"Good gracious! What a lot of obstacles there are to getting married! And I thought it was the simplest thing in the world! Never mind. She shall wear her old tam-o'-shanter then; I like her better in that than in all the veils in the world."

Sister Ignatia covered her eyes with her hand at this suggestion, and both Sisters burst into a peal of laughter. "A bride in a tam-o'-shanter! O Mr. Trevor! You could n't mean it!"

Geoffrey was in a minority. "Well, I did mean it; but Alexia shall do as she pleases about the veil. How long would it take to sew one up?"

Alice had no voice in the matter. She was silent and shy and blushing, and entirely absorbed in the joy of being with Geoffrey again. She kept her brimming eyes fixed upon him; and he, of course, never took his eyes off her. A nice time the Sisters must have had!

The decision was that Geoffrey must wait. He wanted Alice then to go over to see Laura with him. I think he was a little afraid of Laura, and his haste about marriage may have been partly owing to the fact that marriage first, and opposition afterward, was in his mind the best policy. But Alice said he must go first by himself, and he left her with much reluctance.

So it was that Geoffrey came rowing across the harbor alone, and found Mrs.

Trevor and Murray and me in conclave, — holding an autopsy, Murray said. As the boat neared the shore, Murray ran to the veranda-rail, and shouted wildly. As Geoff bounded up the bank, Laura got up from her chair, a great exertion for her, and went down three steps to meet him. He put out his hand, but Laura raised her face to his, and kissed him. This touched Geoffrey very deeply, and for a moment he could n't speak. He patted Laura's hand, and Murray slapped him on the back, and for a minute or two not a word was uttered.

I think it was lucky I had gone over first to pave the way. I sent my card up, with the request that Mrs. Trevor would come down as soon as possible, and she responded by appearing without delay. I had hardly prepared myself properly; for in my intense sympathy for Geoff, and my desire to see him happy, I had forgotten that after all Alice was not the goddess to Mrs. Trevor that she appeared to him and me, and that she might find news of such an alliance as this unpleasant, as well as startling.

"Something has happened to Geoffrey, I am afraid?" she asked anxiously, as she gave me her hand. "He is worse?" She feared that the breaking of his engagement with Helen might have caused a relapse.

"Oh no, no, no," I said, smiling; "he is better; he is well. And he has come down to Quartz to see Alice"—she frowned—"and to ask her to marry him."

To my surprise, Mrs. Trevor burst into a flood of tears. I was unprepared for this, I don't know why, for women may be counted upon to do just what you don't expect them to do. I did n't know what was the matter with her,—whether it was an agreeable shock or otherwise; but she began smiling and talking through her tears. "He ought to do it, of course; it is the only thing. An ill-assorted marriage is to be deplored, and I dread the stir and gossip this will make, especially so soon after that wretched affair with Helen. But I know she will make Geoffrey happy, and he can take her at once away from her surroundings."

"He 'll not do that," I replied. "He is

not marrying her from duty, but because he is madly in love. He does n't dream he is lowering himself; and to tell the truth, I don't think he is. She will exalt him. She is a most uncommon girl."

"Oh, she is!" said Laura, quickly. "I have had her about me a great deal lately, and have been struck by her remarkable sweetness of character. She has been a heroine too. But I wonder what on earth Murray will say!"

Murray said naught for a whole minute, except with his staring eyes and gaping mouth. His first utterance was classic. "Well, I 'll be shot!" he said. "And so he is in love with that girl, after all! Well, then he must marry her, of course. [How I resented that tone in them both!] I thought he had forgotten all about her, I did, truly. But what on earth will the haughty Helen say?"

"She is engaged to Lorimer," I said. "Geoffrey heard it from Steve Gaylord last night; his mother had had a letter from Miss Courtice herself."

"You don't mean it! By Jove! Laura, do you hear that? Well, between 'em they'll keep the tongues at the Club wagging till doomsday. I've hated to go there, actually.

"And so Geoff is going to marry our little fisher maiden!" he went on. "Well, well! doesn't it seem funny, Laura, eh? But, say, though, Lolly, we'll have to move out of this. We never could have old Iron to dinner. Fancy him, will you, handing you in, Laura, and stumbling all over you, in his calico jumper and his ear-rings — and his hat, of course, he never takes off his hat; and 'a-settin' down to supper, Mrs. Tree-vor.'" And Murray roared at the sketch he had drawn. "It makes a complication, doesn't it?" he said, sobering. "I don't think I ever could regard old Iron as a relation, somehow." And he went off in another fit.

Laura could not bring herself to regard it as a joke quite yet. "We've got to face it, Murray," she said, "and to make the best of it, knowing how happy Geoffrey will be, and how lovely and dear Alice really is." And then it was that Murray had spied Geoffrey, and given him the whoop of welcome.

XII.

GEOFFREY, finding his audience eagerly sympathetic, told it his troubles on the marriage question. When he came to the flannel gown and the tam-o'-shanter, Laura burst into wild laughter. "O Geoffrey, Geoffrey, you delicious simpleton!" she exclaimed, nearly choking. "Now let *me* manage this part for you. You do as you're bid. You are to bring Alice directly to us, and let her find her way to the family heart at once. Then I will send to town for things for her ["Oh, why must brides have 'things'?" groaned Geoffrey], and I will have a sweet wedding dress made for her, and you must get out some of your mother's laces, — and O Geoffrey, how lovely she will be in them! — and then, just as soon as we are all ready, you shall be married. But don't dash into things like a wild man, Geoffrey, — I want

Alice to be used to us and our ways before she goes out into the world."

"She's not going out into the world," said Geoffrey, hastily. "I would keep her in a glass case if I could; and don't you instil any worldly wisdom into her, either, Laura, mind. I don't want her to know a thing — or a soul — more than she knows now," he added. "She's perfect as she is."

Geoffrey had been delighted at Laura's mention of Alice's place in the family heart, and it was clear that Laura had at last found her way to his. As soon as dinner was over, he went to fetch Alice. Laura was all impatience to see her, and to remove her from her environments, she confessed to me in a whisper.

Old Iron was struck dumb and silly by the news. Of course he wouldn't and couldn't and didn't believe it; and he went through more labial and lingual contortions in three minutes than he had done in the rest of his life — without being able to squeeze out a syllable! Speech for once was denied him. About a year afterward, — just a week before he died, by

the by, — he told me all about it; how he
felt, I mean. " You see," he said, "that
afternoon I was a-comin' up the plank,
thinkin' o' nothin', as usual, and Alice she
come a-runnin' to meet me. Says she, ,
' Gran'father!' an' says I, ' Wot?' an' says
she, ' I 'm a-goin' to be married — to Mr.
Geoffery,' says she, as suddin as that. I
looked right at her. ' Be you crazy?' says
I, for I look upon them folks as kings an'
queens, Mr. Farley. But Alice she says,
' *It is so,*' says she, an' after a while I *hat*
to believe it! Ef the old woman had n't 'a'
lost her mind long before that, she 'd 'a'
done it then, I guess! But she went on
a-scourin' her pots an' pans jest the same,
when I told her. For years she aint cared
for nothin' but jest keepin' her kitchen
clean."

It was not a connection of which Geoffrey could be proud, but his tact was marvellous, and a prince of the blood could
not have borne himself better.

But this is going leagues ahead of my
story. After Geoffrey had been gone an
hour, and while we were still discussing
the affair of the season, the familiar form

of the green dory was seen making for
" our " little beach ; and Alice, still
blushing and shy, and yet with a sweet
composure of her own, came up the grassy
bank and the steep rock, hand in hand
with Geoffrey. It made an enchanting
picture in the moonlight. Laura took her
in her arms, and called her cousin ; Murray
capered about her like a Newfoundland
dog; and I — well, I behaved as well as I
could outwardly, and inwardly felt a sharp
pang of jealousy, at the thought that Geoffrey would never need me any more.

Alice sat in our midst, the heroine of
the hour. She only smiled at first, and
said yes and no; but after a time she grew
bolder, and talked sweetly and naturally.
Dear Alice! there never was such another. How lovely she did look, sitting
there, with the moon full upon her, giving
her a new radiance ; and with her eyes
upturned to it now and then! And how
handsome Geoffrey was, too, with every
line smoothed out of his face now, and
with perfect peace reigning there!

I think it was pure joy we all felt that
evening, and we shared and shared alike.

Laura seemed younger and fresher and stronger than I had ever seen her ; Murray was his own hearty self, multiplied by two, to suit the occasion ; Geoffrey and Alice need no description ; and I did the benign, bless-you-my-children part, with, I hope, a tolerable grace. Geoffrey and I were of the same age, and had been at college together; but his temperament had made him a son to me.

▸ "I speak to take Alice for her first drive round the suburbs of the city," said Murray. "I drive better horses than he does," he said to Alice, designating Geoffrey, "and I am a far better whip than he, really."

Alice drew a long, rapturous breath. "Ah-h!" she sighed, in delight. "I have never been in a carriage in my life ; you don't begin to know what a Hottentot I am," laughing. "I have never worn a glove, nor carried a parasol. I used to play parasol, when I was a child, with a long stick, which I held up before me ; and I used to make a proud face, as I had seen ladies do." And Alice assumed a little pout, and drew down her eyelids, glancing languidly

from under them. I don't know how this
struck Laura; to us men it was simply
ravishing.

"You know more French than I, and
speak it better," said Laura; "you write a
charming hand, and you play beautifully!"
How Geoffrey blessed her tact. "A fool
can carry a parasol, and it does n't re-
quire more than the average intelligence
to sit behind a pair of horses; does it,
Geoffrey?"

"Oh, but I mean to learn to do everything," she said, nodding her head vigor-
ously, and pursing her red lips. "I can
row, although I know my stroke is too
short," glancing archly at Geoffrey. "It's
the fisherman's stroke. I would n't have
dared try any other here, but I have practised by myself, often."

In the midst of her gayety she grew
pale, and her eyes took on a kind of awed
expression. Geoffrey spoke to her. "I
am afraid of so much happiness," she said,
in answer to his questioning. "I shall
forget all about Heaven."

I was obliged to leave this enchanted
group next morning. I was to be sum-

moned in plenty of time for the wedding,
which was to be in a week or two.

The day came ; or, rather, the night before came first, and I went down to spend
it, for the wedding was to be early in the
morning.

Alice had been with the Sisters for a day
or two ; for, self-contained as they were,
they were desolate at losing her. She endeared every one to her ; even the Trevors'
servants, who probably found the exalta-
tion of old Iron's grandchild a hard pill to
bolt, were won completely by her sweet
graciousness, and scrambled to wait upon
her.

Laura recounted to me many anecdotes
of Alice's management, in her extremely
difficult position, with regard to the townspeople. " She talks freely to them about
her marriage," said Laura, " and they know
that instead of losing an obscure friend,
they are gaining an influential one."

" Where are they going to live ? " I
asked.

" They are to borrow our boat first, for
a cruise, and then Geoffrey has taken a
house over on the Head, which has just

been vacated. He means to buy it later, he says. I hope not, for I anticipate a grand social success — anywhere else — for Alice."

Then they were not to leave the old surroundings! There was not one ray of false pride about either of them.

But the wedding! I need the pen of a painter in words — not this bare reed — with which to depict that. It was a mingling of sunshine and solemnity such as is seldom seen. There were wax-lights and flowers on the altar, and the sunlight danced upon it. As a great surprise to Alice, the Sisters had enlisted a choir from the city; and Alice was so overcome that she could hardly go in to be married, she said. The little boys, in their snowy clothes, whatever the name of them is, came in, in twos, with a tall golden cross leading them, and singing a marriage hymn: " The voice that breathed o'er Eden." Then Geoffrey and I came in, and waited for the bride, whom Geoffrey had not seen for two whole days! She was escorted by Murray, it being voted impossible to pound a scrap of executive ability into the old grandfather, who was there, by the by, in a very nice suit of black, and who kept himself well in the background, being ashamed of his clothes, I suppose.

Laura afterward described Alice's dress to me as a shimmering silk muslin. The Sisters had embroidered it exquisitely, she said. But whatever the dress may have been, or was, Alice was glorious in it. She wore an uplifted, seraphic look ; and her face, which was pale, had taken on an unearthly beauty which none of us will ever forget. She gave no sign of recognition to Geoffrey, who came to meet her with love and rapture in his face, except to drop her eyes ; and it was very evident to us all that she was entering her new estate with a complete sense of its responsibilities.

Even after the ceremony, when the priest shook hands with her, she was perfectly grave ; and I knew she felt herself in a more awful Presence than ours, from the fact that she did not blush or smile. She kept the same far-off, exalted look all the time.

Geoffrey took her hand in his — he did

not give her his arm — and led her from
the chancel; and while the choir sang, the
two went out at the side-door quietly, and
into the Sisters' house, where we hastened
after them.   Then Alice was herself again,
and received our pretty speeches, and her
husband's overwhelming attentions, with
modesty and roses.

But I saw her for weeks — I often see
her now — standing or kneeling at the
altar, with that glorified look she must
have caught from an angel.

A fortnight or so after this, Geoffrey
came springing up my office-stairs.   There
was no need of asking how he was; bliss
was inscribed all over him.   " Come and
be perpetual guest," he cried, "we both
want you, and must have you.   [It was
his kindness; he knew how forlorn I
was without him !]   Don't think I can get
on without you because I am all right,
old boy, any more than I could when I
was all wrong.   And by the by," he
added, "I am coming to study in real
earnest now ; I have promised Alexia to
go to work."

" Get out of my office ! " I shouted. " I liked you when you were cross and sulky and unmanageable ; now you have no attraction for me. If there is a disgusting spectacle on this earth, it is that of a supremely happy man ! "

THE END.

BIOGRAPHIES OF MUSICIANS.

LIFE OF LISZT. With Portrait.

LIFE OF HAYDN. With Portrait.

LIFE OF MOZART. With Portrait.

LIFE OF WAGNER. With Portrait.

LIFE OF BEETHOVEN. With Portrait.

From the German of Dr. Louis Nohl.

In cloth, per volume . . . . $ 1.00
The same, in neat box, per set 5.00
In half calf, per set 12.50

Of the "Life of Liszt," the *Herald* (Boston) says: "It is written in great simplicity and perfect taste, and is wholly successful in all that it undertakes to portray."

Of the "Life of Haydn," the *Gazette* (Boston) says: "No fuller history of Haydn's career, the society in which he moved, and of his personal life can be found than is given in this work."

Of the "Life of Mozart," the *Standard* says: "Mozart supplies a fascinating subject for biographical treatment. He lives in these pages somewhat as the world saw him, from his marvellous boyhood till his untimely death."

Of the "Life of Wagner," the *American* (Baltimore) says: "It gives in vigorous outlines those events of the life of the tone poet which exercised the greatest influences upon his artistic career. . . . It is a story of a strange life devoted to lofty aims."

Of the "Life of Beethoven," the *National Journal of Education* says: "Beethoven was great and noble as a man, and his artistic creations were in harmony with his great nature. The story of his life, outlined in this volume, is of the deepest interest."

Sold by all booksellers, or mailed, on receipt of price, by

A. C. McCLURG & CO., PUBLISHERS,
COR. WABASH AVE. AND MADISON ST., CHICAGO

SHORT HISTORY OF FRANCE,

FOR YOUNG PEOPLE. By Miss E. S. KIRK-
LAND, author of "Six Little Cooks," "Dora's House-
keeping," &c.

12mo, cloth, price, $1.25.

———◆———

"A very ably written sketch of French history, from the ear-
liest times to the foundation of the existing Republic." — *Cincinnati Gazette.*

"The narrative is not dry on a single page, and the little history may be commended as the best of its kind that has yet
appeared." — *Bulletin, Philadelphia.*

"A book both instructive and entertaining. It is not a dry
compendium of dates and facts, but a charmingly written history." — *Christian Union, New York.*

"After a careful examination of its contents, we are able to
conscientiously give it our heartiest commendation. We know no
elementary history of France that can at all be compared with
it." — *Living Church.*

"A spirited and entertaining sketch of the French people and
nation, — one that will seize and hold the attention of all bright
boys and girls who have a chance to read it." — *Sunday Afternoon, Springfield (Mass.).*

"We find its descriptions universally good, that it is admirably
simple and direct in style, without waste of words or timidity of
opinion. The book represents a great deal of patient labor and
conscientious study." — *Courant, Hartford (Conn.).*

"Miss Kirkland has composed her 'Short History of France'
in the way in which a history for young people ought to be written; that is, she has aimed to present a consecutive and agreeable story, from which the reader can not only learn the names of
kings and the succession of events, but can also receive a vivid
and permanent impression as to the characters, modes of life,
and the spirit of different periods." — *The Nation, New York.*

———◆———

Sold by all booksellers, or mailed, on receipt of price, by

A. C. McCLURG & CO., PUBLISHERS,

COR. WABASH AVE. AND MADISON ST., CHICAGO.

TALES FROM FOREIGN TONGUES.

MEMORIES. A Story of German Love. By
MAX MULLER.

GRAZIELLA. A Story of Italian Love. By
ALPHONSE DE LAMARTINE.

MADELEINE. A Story of French Love. By
JULES SANDEAU.

MARIE. A Story of Russian Love. By
ALEXANDER PUSHKIN.

In cloth, gilt top, per volume. $1.00
The same, in neat box, per set 4.00
In half calf or morocco, gilt top, per set 9.00
In half calf or morocco, gilt edges, per set . . . 10.00
In flexible calf or russia, gilt edges, per set . . 12.00

The series of four volumes forms, perhaps, the choicest
addition to the literature of the English language that has
been made in recent years.

Of "Memories," the London *Academy* says: "It is a prose
poem. . . . Its beauty and pathos show us a fresh phase of a
many-sided mind, to which we already owe large debts of
gratitude."

Of "Graziella," the Boston *Post* says: "It is full of beautiful sentiment, unique and graceful in style, of course, as were
all the writings of this distinguished French author."

Of "Madeleine," the New York *Evening Mail* says: "It is
one of the most exquisite love tales that ever was written,
abounding in genuine pathos and sparkling wit, and so pure in
its sentiment that it may be read by a child."

Of "Marie," the Cincinnati *Gazette* says: "It is one of the
purest, sweetest little narratives that we have read for a long
time. It is a little classic, and a Russian classic, too."

Sold by all booksellers, or mailed on receipt of price, by
A. C. McCLURG & CO., PUBLISHERS,
COR. WABASH AVE. AND MADISON ST., CHICAGO.

WE TWO ALONE IN EUROPE.

By MARY L. NINDE. Illustrated from Original Designs.

12mo, 348 pages, price, $1.50.

———◆———

The foreign travels which gave rise to this volume were of a novel and perhaps unprecedented kind. Two young American girls started for " the grand tour " with the father of one of them, and he being compelled to return home from London they were courageous enough to continue their journeyings alone. They spent two years in travel, — going as far north as the North Cape and south to the Nile, and including in their itinerary St. Petersburg and Moscow. Miss Ninde's narrative is written in a fresh and sprightly but unsensational style, which, with the unusual experiences portrayed, renders the work quite unlike the ordinary books of travel.

It is a narrative told so naturally and so vividly that the two gentle travellers do not seem to be " alone," but to have taken at least the reader along with them. . . . It is filled with so many interesting glimpses of sights and scenes in many lands as to render it thoroughly entertaining. — *The Congregationalist, Boston.*

As the work of a bright American girl, the book is sure to command wide attention. The volume is handsomely bound and copiously illustrated with views drawn, if we mistake not, by the author's own fair hands, so well do they accord with the vivacious spirit of her narrative. — *Times, Troy, New York.*

In these days when letters and books about travels in Europe have become generally monotonous, to say the least, it is absolutely refreshing to get hold of a bright, original book like " We Two alone in Europe." . . . The book is especially interesting for its fresh, bright observations on manners, customs, and objects of interest as viewed through these young girls' eyes, and the charming spice of adventure running through it. — *Home Journal, Boston.*

———◆———

Sold by all booksellers, or mailed on receipt of price, by

A. C. McCLURG & CO., PUBLISHERS,

COR. WABASH AVE. AND MADISON ST., CHICAGO.

www.ingramcontent.com/pod-product-compliance
Lightning Source LLC
Chambersburg PA
CBHW022352020726
47500CB00002B/237